RUMOR CENTRAL

RUMOR CENTRAL

RESHONDA TATE BILLINGSLEY

Dafina KTeen Books
KENSINGTON PUBLISHING CORP.
http://www.kensingtonbooks.com

To TLC

(My Teen Advisory Board that keeps me hip)

A note from the author . . .

I love making up stories (my mom calls it lying), but it's really my imagination at work. But I'll be honest, I have been known to take a little truth here, a few facts there, and use them as the foundation for some pretty awesome stories.

That's why when I decided to do the Rumor Central series, I knew I had to draw on my time as a reporter for *The National Enquirer*. Yes, I used to dig up dirt and gossip on celebrities for a living. Needless to say, that was the most interesting job I ever held. But at the end of the day, I decided being a true Gossip Girl wasn't for me. So I turned in my spy card and walked away—but not before amassing some pretty interesting stories. One day, maybe I'll meet you out and about and can share them with you. But for now, I use that experience to craft what I hope is the page-turning story of a teen who makes a name for herself digging up dirt.

I am so excited that you're holding in your hands the first of what I hope will become a must-read series for you. You'll definitely have to let me know what you think. And if you enjoy, make sure you spread the word!

In the meantime, I have to give a quick shout-out to the people that help me do what I do—my wonderful family, my friends, my hard-working agent, Sara Camilli and my wonderful editor, Selena James (I'm just so thrilled to be working with you again). And to the rest of the staff of Kensington, I look forward to making publishing magic!

Thanks also to the thousands of young people who have read, and will read, my books. Those who emailed, tweeted and sent constant messages looking for more teen reading, I hope you enjoy.

Thank you to the parents, teachers, librarians, and concerned adults who are putting these books in their hands. And finally, thank you to my fabulous teen advisory board, that helps me keep it real.

Well, enough from me. Make sure you hit me up and let me know what you think. Now, get to reading!

Much love,

ReShonda

Chapter 1

"*Ain't no party like a Maya Morgan party, 'cuz a Maya Morgan party don't stop!*"

The sounds of the screeching crowd filled The Mansion, Miami's hottest club. Usually reserved for the twenty-one and up crowd, tonight it was closed down just for me!

That's because I got it like that. Just ask any one of the fifteen-hundred people crowded into The Mansion to celebrate my birthday.

Forget Sweet Sixteen, my Sweet *Seventeen* party was one for the history books. MTV was here filming, my reality show *Miami Divas* was taping our season finale, and the deejay had the crowd on their feet, leading them with the chant that everyone was singing.

"*Ain't no party like a Maya Morgan party, cuz a Maya Morgan party don't stop!*"

If I wasn't on top of the world before, I was definitely on it now.

I stood in the VIP box overlooking the dance floor, waving my hands back and forth with the music. My swag was in full force. I was rocking an emerald green Valentino lace tank dress, some five-inch gold Giuseppe Zanotti peep toe pumps and enough jewelry to feed a small village in China. I'd gotten highlights in my jet black, long wavy hair and of course, my makeup was on point.

That's how I roll. My mom says I'm "extra" but I say I'm about that life, that's why when MTV contacted me last year about being on their show "My Super Sweet Sixteen," I told them I was an extraordinary type of girl and I didn't want to do any ordinary type of show. So, I was going to wait a year and do a Sweet *Seventeen* party.

They weren't feeling me at first, but the way the cameraman was panning the hyped up crowd, and the producer was grinning from ear to ear, I knew they were feeling me now.

"Girl, this party is hot!" my friend, Kennedi, said as she bounced to the music. She was rocking a Versace royal blue jumpsuit and looked almost as tight as me. Almost.

"And you thought it wouldn't be?" I laughed as I took another sip of my drink. "You know how I do it."

She laughed, then looked around. "Where's your little crew at?"

I knew it was just a matter of time. Kennedi and I have been friends since we were babies because our mothers had been college roommates. But she lived in Orlando now, so we didn't get to hang as much. For some reason, she didn't cut for my new friends, especially the ones from my reality show *Miami Divas.*

The show starred me and four of my classmates from our private school, Miami High. Don't get it twisted; we weren't your ordinary high school students. If you looked up fab in the dictionary, it would have our picture right next to it. Shoot, Kimora Lee Simmons named her company—Fabulosity—directly after me. (Well, that's my story anyway.) But when you had more money in your purse than most people made in a year, you had no choice but to be fab. And me and my crew were all that and a bag of jalapeño chips.

There was my BFF, Sheridan Matthews. Her mom is world-renowned singer Glenda Matthews. Then, Shay Turner, who can best be described as my frenemy because she's so ghetto-fabulous (and I don't do ghetto) that we clash like oil and water. But her dad, Jalen Turner, is like the biggest basketball player in the country, so she was rolling in dough. The other crew members included Evian Javid, who had more money than all of us combined because her dad is this Middle Eastern billionaire; Bali Fernandez, who I just adore because he is so over-the-top and doesn't care who knows it—including his uptight daddy who is some kind of Cuban diplomat. And then me—you ever heard of the Morgan Hotel chain? That's right, I'm *that* Morgan. Don't hate. Although if you did, I'd be used to it. I'm a five-foot-nine, caramel coated princess. When you put us all together, you had fabulousity at its finest.

I don't know if Kennedi just didn't like the crew or if she was jealous that Sheridan had taken her spot (that's what she always said). So she didn't like the others, but she *despised* Sheridan. And the feeling was mutual.

"They're in the back doing some interviews," I finally said, answering her.

She turned up her nose. "This is about you. Why are they doing interviews?"

I smiled. "Chill, Kennedi. It's all good. My party is going to be part of the season finale."

"I thought this was supposed to just be for MTV."

"They worked out something." I shrugged. I left all those kinds of details to my dad and our attorney.

She finally laughed. "Only you would be able to get MTV to change their whole programming lineup."

"Hey, hey, hey!" my girl Lauren sang as she approached

us. Even though the club was dark, I could tell by the way she was slurring her words that she was high as a kite. Back in the day, me, Kennedi and Lauren were inseparable. But her parents had shipped her off to boarding school and she'd turned into a druggie. Since I don't do druggies, we'd drifted apart. Still, I knew she'd be too through if I didn't invite her to the party, so I'd let her come, but I'd told her to leave all that drug mess alone. Obviously, she didn't listen.

"What's up, girl?" I said, shaking my head at her. She was too pretty to be messing herself up like that. She looked like a younger version of Jada Pinkett Smith and could've been a model or an actress. But now, she stayed too high to do much of anything. "Glad you could make it."

"Sorry I was late. I was ummm, ah . . ." She started giggling.

"Yeah, we know what you were doing," Kennedi snapped. We'd both tried talking to Lauren, but any progress we made with her was lost when she went back to school.

I turned my attention back to the crowd that was now jamming to a TI song. Lauren wasn't about to put a damper on my party.

"Where's your boo?" Lauren asked, looking around the VIP section, which held only about twenty people: my executive producer from *Miami Divas*, Tamara Collins, who also happened to be an old family friend; some MTV executives; my other friends from school, Chenoa, Chastity, and Ava; and a couple of my other close friends.

I smiled as my eyes made their way across the crowded dance floor to my baby, my first love, Bryce Logan. The definition of fine, Bryce had it going on—from his hazel brown eyes to his curly brown hair—he looked like he could be Chris Brown's younger (and much cuter) brother. Bryce's dad played for the Miami Dolphins, and it was his dream to do the same and he was definitely on his way as the star running back at Miami High.

"My boo is over there talking to his friends. I can't wait to see what he got me for my birthday."

"Probably a new BMW," Kennedi joked.

"All I want to know is how can I find me a baller's son?" Lauren said.

"Try saying crack is whack and you might be able to," Kennedi replied.

Lauren looked insulted. "I don't do crack."

"Oh, sorry." Kennedi shrugged and rolled her eyes. "Ecstasy, dope?"

I finally decided to step in. "Hey, you two don't start. This is all about me today."

Kennedi laughed and bumped me, almost making me spill my drink. "Girl, when is it *not* all about you?"

Before I could answer, Sheridan bounced into the VIP area. "Hey, Maya," she said. "Come on, the producers are waiting on you."

Kennedi cut her eyes. "Is Maya the only one you see?"

Sheridan stopped, looked at her, looked around, then turned to Kennedi and said, "Yep." She took my hand and tried to lead me off. "Come on, girl."

I could see Kennedi about to get worked up.

"Chill," I mumbled. The last thing I wanted was any drama at my party. "I'll be right back. Go get a drink. You know my mom is watching the punch like a hawk but I think Carl and his crew have some of the good stuff in the back." I could tell the way Kennedi's nostrils were flaring that she wanted to say something else. But she let it slide.

"Good stuff? I'm coming with you," Lauren threw in.

"I don't know how you can keep being friends with them," Sheridan said as we headed to the back.

I stopped to face her. "Okay, I'm going to tell you like I

told them. Today is all about me. I'm not trying to do the drama, ya feel me?"

"Fine, fine, fine," Sheridan said as she draped her arm through mine and giggled. "Girl, this party is sooo tight!"

I was glad she let it drop as we walked into the back room where they were shooting some scenes from the season finale of *Miami Divas*. The show had done well in our first year on the air. We'd been one of the TV station's highest rated shows.

"If it isn't the fabulous Maya Morgan," Bali said as I walked over to where he and the others stood in a small circle waiting on direction from the producer. Bali was the flamboyant one of the group and today was no exception. He was Versace'd down—from the silk shirt to the skinny jeans. And his Loubutoins were badder than mine.

"You know I'm sick over the shoes," I told him as we air-kissed.

He stuck his foot out and wiggled it. "Eat your heart out, honey. One of a kind." He leaned in closer. "But, missy, I need to talk to you about your guest list."

"What are you talking about?"

"Ummm, yeah, the two Pillsbury Dough girls that have been following me around the party."

I laughed. I knew exactly who he was talking about. "You mean Nina and Tina."

"Nina and Tina, Bina and Kina, whatever. Their names need to be Krispy and Kreme because they look like some fluffy glazed donuts."

"Boy, stop," I laughed.

"Unh-unh. Just a hot mess." He shook his head in disgust.

"Believe me, if I could've left them off, I would have. But they're my cousins."

"Ugh, don't tell anyone else that," Evian added.

"Yeah, you need to get your fam off the buffet table," Shay threw in.

I laughed. Leave it to my crew. You couldn't even tell just 24 hours ago, we were arguing like crazy because they didn't like the idea of filming the season finale at my party because as Shay said, "This show ain't about *her*." But as we always did, we'd worked through our differences. That's because we were a team, in this thing together. And I wouldn't have it any other way!

Chapter 2

The sound of thunder bounced off the walls of the small conference room at WSVV-TV. A Miami storm was brewing outside and it looked like a bigger one was about to jump off inside.

The thunder had to be messing up my hearing, though. Because I just know this one-Reese's-Pieces-away-from-exploding mop head was not saying what I thought he was saying.

"... I'm sorry, I know this may be hard. But we really don't have a choice."

Fired?

Did he really say we were getting fired? *All of us?*

"I know this is not what you wanted to hear. . . ."

It sure wasn't. When Dexter Garrett asked me and my fellow cast members to gather in the conference room at WSVV-TV, I just knew it was to tell us the station executives were caving to our demands. After all, we'd made this little funky no-name channel. It was tanking in the ratings, behind reruns of *The Simpsons*, until we came and did what we do best—shined like the North Star.

Everybody and their dog was talking about *"Miami Divas"*

and after my fab party last week, they hadn't stopped talking about me!

That's why this craziness Dexter was talking wasn't making any kind of sense.

"The season finale taping was great and all, but we've made the decision to go in a different direction," Dexter said.

"Excuse me," Evian said, standing to her feet and tossing her butt-length hair over her shoulder. Every time I saw her do that, I wanted to grab some scissors and cut some of that mess off. I heard those hood girls pay big money for hair like that.

"Yes, Evian?" Dexter said, blowing a long breath like he wasn't in the mood for questions.

"So, you're telling us that *Miami Divas* is no more?" Evian said, waving her Minx nails like they were some kind of magic wand that could make this foolishness disappear.

"What part of *fired* do you not get?" Shay snapped. She had a serious attitude and looked like somebody was about to feel her wrath. But then again, Shay always had an attitude about something.

"I'm sorry," Evian snapped right back. "Where I come from, I don't get fired. My family does the firing."

"Well, you ain't in India no more," Shay huffed, rolling her neck, tossing her honey-blond hair like it was real. "You in Miami, *chica*."

"For the one-thousandth time, I'm not from India! I'm from Dubai. And I don't speak Spanish."

"India, Dubai, Africa, it's all the same." Shay waved her off. Those two were like some old married couple, arguing one minute and best friends the next.

"Hey, Nicki Minaj," Bali yelled at Shay, "can you and Kim Kardashian sit down and let the man finish? Obviously, he has to get to the part where he tells us this is all a joke." Bali raised an eyebrow, turned up his lips, and gave Dexter a "go on" look.

Dexter ran his hands nervously through his hair. "Unfortunately, it's not a joke," he finally said. "Corporate has made the decision not to renew the show."

So *that's* what that crazy conversation from Tamara was about! She'd pulled me aside at the party to ask if I would be interested in my own show. Of course, I told her I would, but she made it seem like that was something for the future. She never said anything about canceling *Miami Divas*, which I definitely couldn't appreciate because she was supposed to be a friend of the family—her aunt and my mom knew each other and she'd interned at my dad's company.

Fired.

I couldn't get that word out of my head. Why would Tamara talk to me about my own show if she was planning on firing me?

"But I thought we were doing great in the ratings." That was Sheridan, speaking for the first time since we gathered in the conference room.

"You were just doing okay," Tamara said, finally speaking up. I should've known something was up since she sat at the head of the table all quiet. She usually called the shots so the fact that she let Dexter begin should've been our cue that this wasn't going to be pretty.

Tamara sighed heavily as she continued. "And well, quite frankly, with the demands you all were making . . ." She let her words trail off. Shay coughed loudly as she shot me the evil eye. She had been completely against us demanding anything, especially because, as she said, "It's not like we needed more money."

But it was the principle of it all. When we'd started the show, it was just a way to highlight our fabulous lifestyle, so we were all in it just for the fun. My dad is actually the one who convinced me that since we had blown up so well the first season, we needed to demand more money and perks and we shouldn't take no for an answer. Everyone had been on board, except for Shay. Now, she was shooting us an "I told you so" look.

Whatever. I wasn't about to take the blame for this. I hadn't held a gun to anyone's head and made them agree with me.

Anyway, I wasn't about to beg for this stupid job. I'd had it going on before this show and I would have it going on after it.

I grabbed my custom-made ostrich Berkin bag, pulled out my Chanel sunglasses, and stood up.

"I don't have time for this," I said. "Maya Morgan doesn't stay anywhere she's not wanted."

Tamara narrowed her eyes at me. "If Maya Morgan would shut up, sit down, and listen—"

"Hold up!" I said, raising my index finger in her direction. "You must think you're talking to some lowlife or something because I'm not the one."

Tamara took a deep breath, then exhaled. "Maya, please have a seat and let us finish."

We faced off. I wondered if I should tell her to kiss my Pilates-toned backside, but up until today, I had liked Tamara, so I let her make it as I slid back into my seat.

"As Dexter was saying," Tamara continued, "we are canceling the show. But . . ." She and Dexter exchanged glances. "We are keeping one of you."

All of us sat straight up.

"What?" Sheridan said.

"You can't do that!" Evian cried.

"We're a team," Bali said.

"Who are you keeping?" I tossed in as my heart raced. Everyone turned around to stare at me, but I didn't care. I needed to know.

"Well"—Tamara hesitated as the room got quiet—"Maya, we'd like to keep you on board to head up the show I was telling you about. It's called *Rumor Central.*"

I wanted to jump up and shout for joy and if I wasn't afraid of breaking my five-inch Louboutins, I would have.

"Oh my God. So, like, what will I be doing?" I wasn't even trying to hide my excitement, even though I could feel the other four shooting me daggers.

"Telling you about?" Sheridan said. "You knew about this?"

"You knew we were getting fired and you didn't say anything to us?" Evian added in disbelief.

I shook my head, but before I could reply, Tamara said, "No, Maya had no idea they were canceling the show."

"That's right. I had no idea," I said with an attitude. How were they getting mad at me?

"But you did know they were looking at you for another show," Bali said, staring at me like he was trying to see straight through me.

"Boy, I was into my party. I didn't know what she was talking about," I snapped. They were really busting my bubble right about now.

"You are such a freakin' liar," Shay said.

"I got your liar," I snapped.

Tamara quickly stepped in. "Look, we are not about to do this," she said with a heavy sigh as she turned back to me. "I just need to know if you're still interested."

I looked around the room and several sets of eyes staring at me. I don't know what they expected me to say, but I knew what I was going to say. "Of course I am!"

"Really, Maya?" Sheridan asked, looking at me like I was crazy.

I stared at her. She was my best friend, but if she wanted to trip with me, I'd let her go in a Miami minute.

I didn't bother answering her; instead, I turned back to Tamara, and whispered, "Maybe we should talk about my new show in another room. I have a feeling this environment is about to get a bit hostile."

Tamara hesitated, then nodded like she knew that was probably best.

"Talk to you guys later," I said, grabbing my purse and getting up from the table.

"Seriously, Maya?" Sheridan repeated.

"You are so foul," Bali said as I headed toward the door.

"With a capital F," Evian added.

"What happened to all that crap you were talking about, 'we're a team. We need to stand together'?" Shay snapped at me, or rather at my back because I was already at the door.

I had given that "we're a team" speech less than twenty-four hours ago, and I'd meant it. At the time. But today was a new day. I was about to get mine and too bad, so sad for my friends.

I turned and shrugged. "Don't hate the player, hate the game," I said, then turned and headed out the door.

Chapter 3

A true diva never lets you see her get excited about anything. But it was taking everything in my power to keep my emotions in check. As the four bigwigs tossed around comments like "all-out promotion," "celebrity interviews," and "hottest show ever," I felt like I was on top of the world. But still, I kept my cool. Honestly, I just wished they'd hurry up and finish so I could go call my boyfriend, Bryce, and tell him the good news. I wondered what kind of gift he'd buy me to celebrate. Bryce loved spoiling me. And getting my own show was definitely cause for spoiling.

"*Rumor Central* will be a hot, new edgy show that will dish the latest celebrity dirt," Tamara said. "I mean, the name is *Rumor Central*, but we just kind of put the rumors out there—you know, in a sensational way. We'll let the people draw their own conclusions. We're like Perez Hilton, Media Takeout, and Bossip on TV—but from a teen perspective. And that's only part of the show. The other is the celebrities coming on, talking about what's hot in their lives, addressing some of the gossip that's going on out there about them, stuff like that."

Tamara eyed me like she was studying me. "So, Maya, are you feeling any of this?" she asked from the head of the table, where she sat with three other executives from the TV station. It had been less than thirty minutes since I'd gotten the news that I'd be getting my own show. But the fact that she'd been able to gather all of these bigwigs so quickly let me know this was serious.

"I mean, you don't seem excited about our plans," she continued.

I yawned like they were boring me, then leaned back and crossed my legs. "Naw, it's cool."

"*Cool?*" Dexter asked. He looked at his colleagues and laughed. They'd filled me in on their plans for me and each word made my heart beat faster and faster. It took a lot to get me excited, but they'd definitely done that.

"So is this even something you want to be a part of?" Dexter asked.

"I told you, I'm cool," I repeated.

One of the executives, who had introduced himself as Mr. Waverly, looked at Tamara with confusion.

"We're rolling out a multimillion-dollar campaign, putting everything we have behind this show, and she says it's *cool?*" he asked.

I didn't need to be ruffling any feathers just yet, so I plastered a smile on my face. "No, I'm totally hyped."

"I can't tell," Dexter mumbled.

"Would you rather she jump up and down like some giddy teenager?" Tamara said, smiling like a proud mother. "She's actually too classy for that, which is why she's the one we chose."

Thank you! Tamara understood me. I knew I liked her for a reason. Divas understood divas.

I leaned forward, tapping my fingertips to emphasize my point. "Let me be clear. I'm totally feeling this and want you to know that you made the best decision by hiring Maya Morgan," I said.

Mr. Waverly narrowed his eyes.

"Do you always refer to yourself in the third person?" he asked me.

I leaned back and smiled. "It's kinda my thing, you know? My trademark. Nicki Minaj has the colored hair, Rihanna has the tats. That's mine." I couldn't be sure, but it looked like he rolled his eyes. I couldn't be concerned with that, though. I had more important issues to clear up. "Now, did I hear someone say something about a clothing allowance?"

"Yes," Tamara replied, "we know you dress well now, but we want to set you up with a new wardrobe, something unique that no one has seen before."

Now that right there was enough to seal the deal. I would never in a trillion years admit this to anyone, but my dad had cut me off. At least temporarily. He said my spending was out of control and we needed to tighten the belt because of the "tanking economy." Please. He was the one always walking around bragging about how we were the "one percent" and we shouldn't be afraid to flaunt it. I wasn't the least bit afraid, and trying to rein me in now was not going to fly.

Tamara turned to a young, pudgy girl who was in desperate need of a makeover and said, "Sonia, can you get with Maya about the wardrobe by tomorrow?"

Sonia nodded and started scribbling on a notepad.

I hoped she wasn't the stylist. If she was, she needed to be fired like yesterday for violating all kinds of dress codes.

Tamara immediately turned back to one of the producers on the other side of her. "Ken, I understand you've snagged a biggie for our first interview?"

The young guy smiled proudly. "Yep, Maya's first interview will be with Sylk."

What? Talk about coming out with a bang. Sylk was the hottest pop star on the planet.

I was just about to comment, but then I thought about something. "If this is supposed to be a gossip show like TMZ, where will we get all the gossip from?" I asked.

"How do you think TMZ gets half the gossip it does?" Dexter answered. "The celebrities themselves plant it. So Sylk is gonna come on, we'll ask a couple of questions about her new album and then she's letting us ask about the beef between her and her record company. Then, we'll be counting on you to help us dig up other dirt on some of the local celebrities."

I was just about to say something else when the conference room door swung open.

"What's going on?" Tamara asked, eyeing the security guard who came running up behind Bali.

"I-I'm so sorry, ma'am," the guard said nervously. "I was trying to lead him out and he took off."

"You doggone skippy I took off," Bali said, transforming into true diva mode. His blond, normally perfect hair was all over his head as if he'd been running. He darted to the other side of the room, away from the security guard. "I'm not leaving out of here until I have my say." He motioned wildly up and down the table. "All of you are low-down. Dirty. For the past two years, we've put our lives on display. My whole stupid country has turned against me because of the shame I brought, but I let you shine a mirror on me for the sake of ratings and this is how you repay me?" he shouted.

"Bali, I understand you are upset, but this is not the time or the place," Tamara calmly said.

"And this little skank right here," he continued, ignoring Tamara and pointing at me.

"Bali, chill. . . ." I began. Maybe I could reason with him since he was the one I was closest to, next to Sheridan.

He jabbed his long, bony finger in my direction. "Look, you little backstabbing troll. If you knew what's good for you,

you would not want to say a word to me because I'm two seconds from stomping that pretty right off your face."

"Whatever," I said, rolling my eyes and leaning back. So much for that idea. I knew there was no talking to Bali when he was this upset, so I just dropped it. Let security deal with it. Bali was a bonafide fool and the last person I wanted to be tussling with was him, especially when he was mad like this.

"You think you Miss High and Mighty, like your stuff don't stink." He held his nose. "Well, boo-boo, I got news for you. It does and when I'm done, everybody will smell it."

I couldn't get why he was so mad at me. I didn't go looking for this job. I guess I was supposed to say, "No, thank you. I'm gonna pass on this opportunity of a lifetime because I don't want to hurt my friends' feelings"?

"Do I have to endure this?" I said, turning to Tamara. "I mean, really, what kind of bootleg joint are you running that you can't keep the riffraff out."

"She's right," Tamara said, standing up and motioning to the guard by the door. "Get him out of here."

The security guard grabbed Bali by the arm. "Oh, this ain't over, boo-boo!" he yelled as they dragged him out. "You got to show yourself at school!"

The execs looked at Tamara in shock. She must've felt compelled to explain. "That's one of the people we just cut. He's a little upset, but he'll be okay."

I knew Bali wasn't the only one who was upset and I could only imagine what the others had to say. "So now I have to walk around in fear of my life?" I asked.

"You know Bali is harmless. He's all talk," Tamara said.

"Well, like Mr. Waverly said, you're investing a lot of money in me." I motioned up and down my body. "And now, I'm even more valuable than I already was. So can I get some protection?"

Tamara let out an uneasy laugh. "So, now you want a bodyguard?"

"Bodyguard, private security, whatever you want to call it, at least until these fools stop tripping with me because I'm sure you don't want anything to happen to me. The liability could be ridiculous." I crossed my toned legs, folded my arms, then gave them a look that said, *I may only be seventeen, but I'm all about the business.*

Dexter rolled his eyes like I was more trouble than I was worth, but I didn't care. Last year, when one of the jocks had made the mistake of teasing Bali for acting like a girl, Bali did a karate chop to his throat, then turned him over and spanked him like he was five years old. So I knew what he was capable of and I wasn't trying to go there.

"Fine," Tamara said. She turned to Pudgy Girl again. "Can you look into that, Sonia?" The girl nodded and once again began scribbling.

"Thank you." I put my Chanel sunglasses on and stood. "Now, this whole situation has me rattled and I need to go clear my head at the spa. But let me say I'm super psyched to be your new host. I'm sure you all can work out all the minor details about my increase in pay and all my perks and get the contract over to my attorney." I flashed a huge smile. "This is all so fab."

"We're not done," Dexter said.

"Just shoot me an email about what else you guys talk about. I have to go let my crew work their magic if you want me ready for a photo shoot. My hairdresser stays booked four weeks in advance, so I'm already calling in favors to get him to see me," I replied.

"We have a hairdresser," Ken said.

I looked at him like he'd lost his mind. He must not have known I'd seen the station's hairdresser at work. If I wouldn't let that Sally Beauty School reject touch my hair for *Miami Divas*, what in the world made him think I was going to do it now.

"Sorry," Tamara said with an apologetic smile. "She doesn't let anyone but her own hairdresser work on her hair.

I ignored all the strange looks on the executives' faces and tossed my purse over my shoulder.

"Talk to you guys later. Smooches," I said, before heading out the door, first to call my boo, then to get my hairdresser, Davion, to hook me up. I couldn't help but laugh as I walked out the door. Miami definitely wasn't ready for the new me!

Chapter 4

I stood at the massive entrance to the school and took a deep breath. Everyone was rushing to class since the bell was going to ring in a few minutes. The teachers at Miami High could seriously trip over tardies. You'd think with all the money our parents paid, they'd give us a little flexibility. I swore they didn't because of the stupid scholarship kids that went here. Some do-gooder thought it would be a great idea to give scholarships to needy students so they could "take part in the private school experience." Personally, I thought it just brought down our stock, but I just stayed away from them and they stayed away from me.

I ran my fingers through my curls, tossed my hair over my shoulder and headed inside. I immediately spotted Chenoa and Sheridan walking down the hall. They didn't see me, but I stopped in my tracks to give them time to go ahead. The last thing I felt like doing was getting into it with anyone. I was too pretty to beef, especially since Davion had worked his magic and I was runway ready. Oh, who was I kidding? I was always runway ready.

Not only was I looking good, but I was feeling good. As

expected, Bryce had shown up last night to take me out to dinner to celebrate. He'd even surprised me with a Tiffany charm bracelet. He must've gone straight to Tiffany's after I called him and told him my good news. That was my boo, he was so thoughtful.

So, obviously, I was floating on cloud nine, sporting my new bracelet and my fabulous 'do and I wasn't trying to let anyone spoil my mood. But, Maya Morgan didn't run from anyone. So, while I briefly thought about staying home so I didn't have to see my former crew, I quickly tossed that thought aside. I needed to be at school and show my face so everyone could see that I was about to become a bigger star than I already was.

As I'd thought, word must've already spread because several people started looking my way as I made my way inside. Many of them were whispering and pointing. I had just made it to my locker when one of the jocks walked over and said, "What's up, Maya. Is it true that you're getting your own TV show?"

"It is," I said, smiling as I threw my calculus book (which I hadn't bothered to open in preparation of my test today) in my locker. "I'm about to blow up on so many levels."

"Wow, that's tight," he said.

"It's messed up, is what it is," Shay said, appearing from nowhere. "But what else can you expect from a backstabbing troll?" She had her usual attitude as she folded her arms like I was supposed to be scared.

I slowly shut my locker and turned to face her. Of course, Evian and Bali were standing behind her, and Chenoa and Sheridan walked up as well. They looked like some kind of gang standing there staring at me. But I wasn't about to be punked, so I smirked.

"Actually, it's pretty nice," I replied. "You should hear all the plans they have now that they got rid of dead weight and have something they can really work with."

Bam! They should know better than to come at me the wrong way. Shay took a step toward me, but Evian cut her off, stepping in front of her to stop her.

"Naw, Shay, let her make it—for now," she said.

Sheridan stepped up. "So out of order," she said.

Sheridan and I faced off like some cowboys from those old Western movies. If she was trying to look intimidating, she needed to take that mess to someone who didn't know her.

"I mean, you don't feel any kind of shame about selling us out?" Sheridan finally asked.

I rolled my eyes. Sheridan was my girl. We'd been friends since seventh grade so I really didn't like beefing with her. "Look," I said, trying to appear sympathetic, "I get that you guys are salty about how all of this went down. I mean, it's messed up how they did this, but seriously, if you were in my shoes, what would you have done?"

Sheridan looked away because she was just like me. She could front all she wanted, but at the end of the day, she would've done exactly what I had.

All this drama was making my head hurt. Kennedi had been ecstatic when I called and told her the news about me getting my own show. That's the way true friends should be. I guess this whole situation was showing me who my friends really were.

"So you knew all along that they were trying to get rid of us and keep you?" Evian asked.

"I told you, I had no idea," I replied. "Tamara just asked if I wanted my own show. I thought she was talking about one day." Suddenly, I was glad that I'd never told them about my connection to Tamara. She'd told me not to tell anyone when we first started the show, just to avoid any problems. I'm glad I listened because that would've been major drama.

"You are such a liar," Shay said.

I gave her the hand. I wasn't about to sit up and try to

convince them that this wasn't some underhanded plot by me to get my own show. They could believe what they wanted to believe.

"Maya, I can't believe you'd do something so foul," Chenoa said. I rolled my eyes at her. Why was she even here? This didn't even have anything to do with her.

"We get that this is business," Bali added. "But you just threw us under the bus. They said, 'we want to keep you,' and you didn't negotiate or anything. Just told us, 'Deuces, I'm out,' without even thinking twice about us."

I raised an eyebrow and shot him a *your point would be?* look.

Shay stepped back in my face. "What makes this so jacked up is that you're the reason we were in this mess in the first place. It was your bright idea to fight for more money, more perks." She paused and tilted her head. "Now that I think about it, maybe you were running game all along. This probably was your plan."

It wasn't, but it dang sure would've been had I thought about it. All is fair in love and reality TV. But since a small crowd was gathering and I wasn't in the mood for drama, I didn't say what I was actually thinking. Instead, I said, "Look, they told me they were planning to cut *Miami Divas* anyway," I lied. "So it had nothing to do with our demands."

"Bull," Bali said.

"You don't have to believe me." I shrugged. "I don't have a reason to lie to you."

"Really, you do," Evian said. "Because what you did was low-down."

Several people had now gathered around like they were ready for something to jump off. The bell rang and nobody moved. I guess seeing a fight was worth getting a tardy.

I let out a long, frustrating breath. See, this was why I needed a bodyguard. I could tell Tamara didn't really think I needed one, which was why she said she would 'look into it'.

But I was going to let her know it's mess like this why I did. But for now, I was on my own. Forget being nice. They wanted drama, I could definitely give it to them.

"If I were you, I'd be nice to me. Because maybe, just maybe I will put in a good word and let you make an appearance on my show," I told them.

"Don't do me any favors," Bali snapped, raising his voice.

"Yeah, screw you and your show," Shay said. She was now all up in my personal space again.

"And tell me again, why are you in my face?" I said, turning up my nose. "And you need a Tic Tac or something because your breath is aggravating my allergies."

"Oooh, I wouldn't take that," someone yelled.

"Clock that chick in the eye," someone else chimed in.

Were they really trying to get a fight to jump off? I hoped not because I didn't fight. I sued. And if any one of them laid a hand on me, I would have my dad's attorney up at the school before they got to their next class.

"Come on, Shay. She's not worth it," Evian said, taking Shay's hand and pulling her back. "Now that we know what kind of backstabber she really is, she doesn't have to ever worry about being our friend again."

I stared at both of them, not blinking. "Can someone pass me some tissue so I can dry my tears?" I said, my voice full of sarcasm.

Several people busted out laughing. I wondered where the heck were the teachers. Usually, when the bell rang, someone was in the hallway ushering us all to class.

Evian tugged at Shay, while Bali and Sheridan just glared at me. "Come on, I told you, she's not worth it. She's gonna get hers."

"Yeah, and I'm gonna be the one to give it to her," Shay snapped.

I really didn't understand why they were trippin' with me. Any one of them would've done the exact same thing.

Shay snatched her arm away, then stepped back in my face. "Payback ain't pretty," she said, spit flying from her mouth.

"Neither is your face," I said, turning to walk off. I wasn't about to do this with them. But I hadn't taken a step when Shay grabbed my hair and yanked me back.

"Owww," I screamed. Before I knew it, I turned around and pushed her as hard as I could. She stumbled back, caught her balance, then came charging toward me, slamming into me like a linebacker on the football team. She then grabbed my six-hundred-dollar freshly done hair as tight as she could and tried to fling me to the floor. Of course, I wasn't going to let it go down like that. So, I grabbed her hair right back and tried to throw her down.

"Let me go!" she screamed.

"You let me go!" I shouted back.

We started rolling around on the floor and all I could think was, *Am I really fighting in my four-inch* Manolo Blahniks?

"Have you two lost your mind?" Mr. Carvin, the school principal, said, racing to break us up. He grabbed Shay by the arm and the softball coach grabbed me.

"I'm gonna kill her!" Shay yelled.

"In your dreams!"

"Stop this fighting, now!" Mr. Carvin shouted as both of us tried to break free.

It took a minute, but we both stopped squirming enough for them to let us go.

"What in the world is your problem? I thought you two were friends," Mr. Carvin yelled.

"Were as in past tense," I said, checking my clothes to make sure that my Juicy Couture jumpsuit hadn't been messed up.

"I was never her friend," Shay snapped, trying to catch her breath. "We just had a show together."

"Whatever. You'd just better get your dad to get his credit card ready," I said, pulling out my rhinestone-studded iPhone.

"Got me up here fighting like some thug," I huffed. "I don't think so! I'm suing you, your mama, your daddy, the whole Miami Heat," I said as I punched in the code to unlock my phone.

Mr. Carvin exhaled in frustration. "Miss Morgan, put that phone away and get in my office right now." I ignored him and kept punching. He actually stepped in front of me and snatched the phone out of my hand.

"Hey, I'm entitled to one phone call," I said.

"This isn't jail," he said, scuttling us into his office.

I cut my eyes at Sheridan, who stood off to the side, watching everything. I was stunned that she hadn't tried to jump in and help me. No matter how many fights we'd had in the past, at the end of the day, she always had my back. Truthfully, I knew Sheridan wasn't a fighter either, but she knew Shay was crazy and she hadn't lifted a finger. She rolled her eyes at me and walked off. Oh, I would definitely never forget that.

Inside Mr. Carvin's office, I immediately began protesting. "Why am I in trouble? She started it by grabbing my hair."

"I didn't grab your hair," Shay said innocently as she plopped down in the chair in front of his desk. "When you walked off, it got caught in my bracelet." She held her arm and shook her dangling bracelets.

"You are such a liar," I yelled.

"Both of you be quiet! Sit down, Miss Morgan!"

"She started it!" I said, sitting down in the seat next to her. "I didn't do—"

"I don't care who started it," Mr. Carvin said, interrupting me as he walked behind his desk. "There is no fighting in this school and you know that this is absolutely unacceptable. You two are seniors. I would expect more from you." He pulled out a notepad. "As you know, we have a zero tolerance for fighting—"

"But—" I said.

"But nothing." He scribbled on the notepad, then handed it to me and Shay. "You both are suspended for three days."

"You can't do this," Shay said, knocking over the chair as she stood.

Mr. Carvin frowned in her direction. "Miss Turner, try me if you want to. I'll change that suspension to the rest of the year and you'll find yourself repeating the twelfth grade."

She rolled her eyes as she took her suspension notice. "Can I go now?" she said, glaring at him.

He nodded. "You need to leave campus immediately," he called out as she stomped toward the door.

She stopped and spun around. "Bu-But, I have a dance competition today and we leave right after school."

"You won't be taking part in anything related to Miami High for the next three days," he replied with a firm tone. "Good day, Miss Turner."

Shay glanced over at me. "You are so going to regret this," she muttered in my direction.

"Whatever, Shay. You started it," I said, before taking my notice and leaving as well.

I noticed this nerdy chick, Valerie Elgin, sitting in the front office, like she was waiting to see someone. Valerie was one of the scholarship students. She was a year younger than us and I only knew her because we used to work on the school newspaper together—back before I came to my senses and quit.

"You okay?" she asked as I walked out of the office. When I didn't answer, she added, "If you ever need anything, I can help." I stopped and stared at her to see was she serious. She must've been because she kept talking. "I mean. . . . I didn't mean. . . . I mean, I know you have a lot going on and I was just thinking . . . if I could help in any way, like with school-work or anything else, I will."

I rolled my eyes at her. "How 'bout you get you some business and stay out of mine."

I put my sunglasses on and strutted out of the building. I sent Bryce a text to pick me up at my house, not after school like we'd planned.

Mr. Carvin just didn't know, this wasn't a suspension. This was a three-day vacation and I was about to make the best of it!

Chapter 5

Whoever thought a suspension was a bad thing definitely didn't know what they were talking about. I sipped my latte as I leaned back in my chair and popped open my sleek Mac-Book Pro. I'd chilled and watched TV all day yesterday. I'd called to check in and Tamara had asked that I do some research on story ideas, so I was cruising all the top gossip sites as I chilled at home. This was the life I'd needed. Bryce had even stopped by after school, so I'd gotten a chance to chill with him.

My email dinged and I groaned when I saw the email from my calculus teacher.

*Miss Morgan, your failure to make up this exam has
resulted in a zero on your test. Normally, we don't allow
students to make up work missed during a suspension, but I
am making this rare exception. Please see me immediately
upon your return to school.*

I closed out the email. It was a good thing I missed the test because I probably would've flunked anyway. I logged onto Twitter and immediately saw that one of my tweets had been retweeted by Valerie Elgin. I didn't even realize she was following me. I hesitated. Maybe seeing her name was some kind of sign. I needed to get some help with my schoolwork and I knew Valerie was just the nerd to do it. I clicked on her name and quickly sent her a direct message asking her to call me. I hated even having to talk to her. But she'd offered and I couldn't flunk this stupid test.

I had just gone back to my gossip sites when my mother came in. She was wearing her short tennis outfit, displaying her long, lean legs. She had her wavy hair pulled up into a ponytail and actually looked like she should be in a tennis commercial. Of course, there was no indication that she'd been playing tennis because the outfit was sparkling white. But knowing my mom, she'd probably hit the ball twice, then sat down to watch as she sipped a Bloody Mary.

"What are you doing at home?" she asked.

I sighed. Usually my mom stayed gone all day, so I hadn't expected her back so soon. I hadn't told her or my dad about the suspension, although I was going to have to before I returned because I wouldn't be allowed back without a parent/teacher conference. But I'd wanted to wait until the last day. I mean, why give them more time to gripe than necessary?

"Uh, I just wasn't feeling well," I said.

"So now I'm raising a liar?" she said.

"What?"

"You got suspended," she stated.

My eyes grew wide. "Huh?" I stammered. How did she find out? I was trying to get my story together, but she stopped me when she held up a piece of paper.

"This email says you were suspended!"

I groaned. Of course the school would send an email letting my mother know about my suspension.

"You got suspended, Maya?" My mother waved the letter like she simply couldn't believe it. "For fighting? Like some common thug?"

"I was defending myself after I was attacked," I said. "Shay Turner jumped me."

She tossed the paper on my dresser and darted toward me.

"Oh my God, you were jumped? Why in the world do I have you in that expensive private school if you have to worry about getting attacked?" She studied my face like she was checking for bruises. "I just can't believe this. Why didn't you tell me?"

"I didn't want to worry you or dad." I took a deep breath and acted like I was fighting back tears. "It was just so horrible."

Dang, I was good. I don't know why Hollywood was sleeping on me.

My mother stroked my hair. "My poor baby. Are you okay?" She pulled back and started examining my face some more.

"I'm fine. Just a little bruised up."

"Do we need to call the doctor?" She turned my cheek, studying me closer.

"I . . . I just couldn't believe that happened and I didn't want to tell you and get you upset."

"This is just ridiculous." She paused like she was thinking. "I knew this would happen when they decided to let those people go to that school."

I hated to bust her bubble, but I said, "It wasn't one of the scholarship kids. It was Shay Turner."

"Wait a minute. Shay Turner. Is that the girl from the show with you?"

I nodded. "Yeah, the one from *Miami Divas*. She was mad because she got fired and they kept me." My parents had been completely behind by new job. My dad's attorney was the one who had worked out all the details in my contract. But none of them knew how upset my former crew was about being fired.

"Jalen Turner's daughter?" my mom asked.

"Yes."

Her mouth dropped open. "Oh, I don't think so," she exclaimed. "I never did like that ol' tattooed-up gangsta. That's what happens when common folks come into money, they don't know how to act. That thug and his ghetto daughter have messed with the wrong woman's child!" she continued.

My mother had made no secret that while she had no problem with the other members of the whole *Miami Divas* crew, she had never been feeling Shay. Even though Mr. Turner was one of the most talented players in the NBA, he was always getting in some kind of trouble.

"That's what I told them, Mom," I said, egging her on. If she was mad at them, she wouldn't be trippin' with me. "I told them I don't fight, I sue."

My mother patted my cheek. "I taught you well, sweetheart." She stood up tall and brushed down her skimpy tennis skirt. "I'm going to talk to your father. We're going to have Daniel get right on this," she said, referring to our family attorney.

I smiled appreciatively. "Thanks, Mom. And don't worry, Tamara is supposed to be looking at getting me a bodyguard." I made a mental note to call her tomorrow to ask her the status on that. I knew the bodyguard wouldn't be allowed at school (Bali's dad had tried to get him a bodyguard once and the school nixed it), but I still wanted one for when I wasn't at school.

I knew my dad would take it over from here, but at least I'd gotten my mom off my back for a while. "Well, I'm just sitting here trying to study so I don't fall behind on any of my work," I said, motioning toward my laptop.

My mother stood and smiled. "That's my baby. Let me let you get back to work. I'll go tell Sui to fix you your favorite food for dinner to make you feel better."

"All right, Mom."

"I love you, sweet pea."

"Love you, too," I replied with a pouty smile as she left my room. I couldn't help but laugh. I was such a great actress. Trust, it was just a matter of time before everybody knew my name!

Chapter 6

It wasn't easy being hated, but somebody had to be the object of jealousy. That was why I eased my sunglasses on my face, and strutted down the hall like I was Tyra Banks at a runway show. Someone had actually put a rat in my locker. A stinking, dirty, filthy rat! It was the most disgusting thing I'd ever seen. Luckily, I didn't scream because I didn't touch it. I opened my locker and the thing was just hanging there. The custodian said I was being dramatic because it was really just a small lab rat from one of the biology classes, but a rodent is a rodent. I made them fumigate my locker. Of course, nobody saw anything when I asked, but I knew who was behind it.

I was just ready to get out of there because in addition to that rat foolishness, I was tired of dealing with the hate and nasty looks and I definitely wasn't trying to get into it with Shay again.

I walked over to my car and stopped in my tracks at the sight of my prized silver BMW 750 sitting on four flat tires.

"Oh my God! What happened to my car?" I screamed.

A group of people were standing nearby, including Evian, Bali, Shay, and Sheridan. I spun toward them. "What happened to my car?" No one answered. "I know you did this," I said, pointing at my former friends.

"I don't know what you're talking about," Evian said, trying to look innocent.

Bali just smirked, and Sheridan and Shay just stood there grinning and looking stupid.

"One of you did this to my car," I said, jabbing my finger in the direction of the tires. "My tires are jacked up!"

Bali's hand went to his chest. "Oh my goodness. I hadn't even noticed." He then turned to Evian. "Did you see who did this?"

Evian shook her head as she shrugged innocently. "I sure didn't." She turned to Shay. "Did you?"

"Nope," Shay replied, then blew a gigantic bubble with her gum.

Cow.

They all looked at Sheridan, like they were really waiting for an answer.

"I didn't see anything either," Sheridan said with a tight smile. "But that's so messed up that someone would do that."

"Because you of all people don't deserve anything like that," Evian added.

"It sure is messed up," Bali said, like he was really concerned. "And didn't you just get a whole new set of tires?"

I ignored him and turned to another one of my classmates, who was standing around gawking. "What about you? Did you see who did this?"

He, too, just stared at me like he was stuck on stupid, while everyone around him started giggling.

They made me so sick. "Did you see who did this?" I asked, turning to another one of my classmates who was standing nearby. He gave me a look like even if he had, he wasn't saying a word.

"Whatever," I finally said when it was obvious they

weren't going to tell me anything. "Do you think this is gonna stop me?" I shouted to no one in particular. "All of you are just mad. Don't think I'm not gonna find out who did this!"

"Good luck with that," Shay said, laughing.

"I have a major meeting in," I glanced at my watch, "an hour and your stupid, childish behavior is gonna make me late!"

Shay shrugged. "Guess your little show is just gonna have to wait."

It was moments like this that I wished I had some male thug cousins or something because I would get one of them to straight jack Shay up.

"Whatever. Screw all of you," I said, pulling my phone out of my purse. I stopped ranting and faced my former crew. "Hate isn't a good look," I said, finally calming down. I was just about to punch in Bryce's number when he walked up.

"Hey, what's wrong with you?" he asked when he saw the disgusted expression on my face.

"Someone put my tires on flat. All four of them," I said, trying not to get worked up. I needed to let these busters know they couldn't faze me.

"What?" he said, eyeing my car. "Who did it?"

I pointed at Shay and her stupid flunkies. "One of my deranged stalkers did it, I'm sure," I said.

"Honey boo-boo, you'd be the last person I'd ever stalk," Bali said.

"I can't tell." I didn't give them a chance to respond as I turned back to Bryce. "Look, can you take me home? I was just about to go call you."

"Yeah. . . . Ummm, I'm sorry . . . but . . ."

"But what?" You could've knocked me over with a feather when Bryce hesitated, looked at me, then at Sheridan, then back at me.

"But"—he took a deep breath and lowered his voice—
"but, I need to talk to you." He took my arm and tried to
lead me away. I jerked my arm from his grasp.

"Talk to me about what?" I snapped.

He looked down, then over at Sheridan again.

"Boy, if you don't say what you need to say . . ." I began.

He let out a deep sigh, then softly said, "I think we kinda
need to chill a while."

Are you freakin' for real? I wanted to scream. Just yesterday
he was talking about how much he loved me. Now he was
seriously about to flake out on me?

Bryce cleared his throat and looked uneasily at Sheridan,
who was glaring at him. I looked back and forth between the
two of them. I was about to ask Bryce what in the heck was
going on when his teammate Wade walked up.

Without even looking at me, Wade said, "Dude, you're seriously still talking to her after what you found out?"

My hands went to my hips and my eyebrows rose. "What
is he talking about, Bryce?"

Bryce shot Wade some kind of look that I couldn't make
out, then said, "Would you let me handle this?"

Wade shook his head, then gave me a disgusted look as he
walked off.

Since I couldn't care less about that nobody Wade, I didn't
pay him any attention. But I did care about Bryce and if someone had told him something, I wanted to know what it was.

"Bryce, what is he talking about?"

Bryce looked at Sheridan again and I swear she was glaring at him. He took my arm and pulled me to the side, away
from everyone.

"Look, Maya," he said. "I've just been thinking about this
and I think you're cool and all, but I think we need to chill."

"Excuse me?" I said, stunned. *No, this fool wasn't breaking
up with me.* Nobody broke up with Maya Morgan! Maya
Morgan was the one who did the breaking up.

"It's just that . . ." Bryce paused, looked nervously around, then continued. "It's just that, I heard some things and . . ."

Now, normally, I would've just told Bryce where he could go, but the look on his face had me curious. "What is it you heard, Bryce?"

He hesitated again, then rushed his words out. "I heard you got with Kenny—and his boy, Dave, at the same time."

"What?" I exclaimed. I was shocked—for two reasons. One, because I *did* get with Kenny last year. Kenny was Bryce's former teammate and Miami High's resident bad boy, who'd been kicked out of school last year because he was always getting into trouble. We'd hooked up—in one serious lapse of judgment moment. And number two, because I couldn't for the life of me figure out why Bryce would think me of all people would kick it with two guys at the same time.

"Are you freakin' kidding me?" I said. "You're seriously going to come at me with this mess?"

Bryce gritted his teeth. "I talked to Kenny's brother. He said it's true. And then I heard from a reliable source that Dave was with him."

I looked around like I was waiting for Ashton Kutcher to jump out the bushes and tell me I was being punk'd or something.

"I never got with his friend. I don't even know anyone named Dave!"

He stopped and stared at me. "So you did get with Kenny then?" he asked, disgusted.

I couldn't believe I'd set myself up like that. But I understood his disgust. Not only was Kenny Bryce's former best friend, even though it was back when they were in middle school, but Kenny had a major reputation for talking to any girl that gave him the time of day—short, tall, fat, skinny, ugly, pretty, Kenny didn't care and it had earned him a horrible reputation. So any girl worth anything wouldn't be caught dead with him. So why had I given him the time of day? Let's just say that was the first and last time I'd ever had something to drink at a party. But that was long before Bryce, so what difference did it make?

"Who told you I got with Kenny?"

"It doesn't matter," he replied.

"Where did you get that from, Bryce?" I repeated.

He didn't have to answer. I knew who had told him. The only other person who knew about me and Kenny, my former BFF—or should I say my enemy because Sheridan telling my business like that meant it was about to be on!

"Look, who told me doesn't matter. Just the fact that I know you've been with Kenny makes me sick to my stomach. Nobody wants one of Kenny's exes as their girl. I can't even . . ." He shook his head like he couldn't even finish his sentence.

"I'm not Kenny's ex!" I said firmly. Then I caught myself. I was so not about to stand out here and plead with a guy to be with me. Maya Morgan didn't roll like that.

I stood straight and let my attitude show all over my face. "You believe what you want to believe," I said. "But a word of advice. I wouldn't be listening to jealous has-beens who wish they could be me."

"I mean, if it's not true, maybe . . ."

I gave him the hand to stop talking to me. Forget Bryce. Not only had he been ready to assume the worst, but he was going to break up with me over it? Oh, I don't think so.

"Bryce, go crawl back under your rock," I said. "I am so done talking to you. Forever."

Sheridan just didn't know—this little move marked the beginning of an all-out war!

Chapter 7

I breathed a sigh of relief as the black Porsche pulled up to the curb. I had called Tamara to tell her I'd be late for the meeting we had this afternoon and thankfully, she was out running an errand and agreed to just swing by and get me on her way to the station. I didn't even feel like dealing with my car with all those idiots standing around gawking. My dad would just have to send someone for it later. Right now, I just wanted to get away from this stupid school before I hurt somebody.

"So, you had a bad day, huh?" Tamara asked after I had climbed into her front seat. I really liked our relationship. Even though she was technically my boss, she acted more like my big sister. She told me it was because she felt a connection to me, probably because I reminded her of herself at seventeen. I didn't know about all that, but Tamara was definitely cool people. I mean, how many other bigwigs would drop everything and come when I called. Not to mention, she was the baddest dresser (outside of me) that I knew.

I leaned back in the soft seat. "That's the understatement of the year."

"I hate to hear what happened," she said as she navigated her luxury vehicle onto the freeway. "What are you going to do about your car?"

I'd told her that I thought one of my *Miami Divas* co-stars had something to do with putting my tires on flat, but I couldn't prove it.

"My dad will take care of it," I replied. I just wanted to get away. If we didn't have this meeting at the station, I would've had Tamara take me straight home. I'd never admit it out loud, but I was actually pretty sad about Bryce.

"Look, I know you're bummed—"

"I'm not bummed," I said, cutting her off, it's just a stupid car. I didn't want Tamara thinking I was giving my ex-friends the satisfaction of upsetting me.

"Well, I'm just telling you to keep your eye on the big picture," she said with a huge smile.

"And what would that be?" I said. I turned and stared out of the window. I didn't know what I was feeling more—mad at my former crew, or hurt over Bryce. Either way, none of them would ever know. I was planning on keeping it diva style. I'd never be reduced to fighting again. That reminded me, I hadn't told Tamara about the fight. But the way she was rambling, I just decided not to say anything, period. It was over and done with anyway.

"I mean, just imagine the looks on all of their faces when they see your new show. Everyone is going to be sick to see how much you've blown up."

Tamara knew just what to say to me. I was feeling better already. I finally smiled and she patted my hand.

"Maya, you were meant for this," Tamara continued. "Don't let any of this petty high school drama get you down. You're about to be on a whole other level." She paused as she pulled into the parking lot at the television station, swiped her key card, and went through the gate. "We are about to make this show one of the hottest, freshest young shows that America has ever seen. And when you blow up as the host, all your so-called friends will be green with envy."

"The source of their envy is plain to see, they'll be hating because they can't be me," I softly mumbled.

"What?" Tamara looked at me strangely.

I shook my head. "Oh, nothing. That's just something me and Sheridan used to say."

Tamara parked in her reserved spot, then turned off the car. "Well, you won't just be saying it. You're now about to be living it."

I liked the way she talked.

"So, you got some show ideas?" she asked as we made our way into the building.

"I do," I replied. "I didn't get as much research done as I wanted because I have this stupid calculus class that is kicking my butt, and I missed a test that I know my teacher is going to be trippin' about." I sighed heavily. I couldn't wait for graduation.

"Why don't you get a tutor? The station will pay for it." Tamara's eyes lit up like an idea had just come to her. "It would be great if you could get someone from your school to tutor you and assist you when necessary. You don't have any geeks at your school looking for a part-time job?"

Part-time? I needed help full-time if they wanted me to maintain my fabulosity, but I didn't push it—yet.

"I did have this girl from my school help me get ready for this test."

Of course, Valerie had quickly responded to my Twitter message. She'd come by the next day and done a crash course on the calculus test, which she'd already taken. It was grueling, but I took the makeup exam this morning and I felt like I'd done all right.

"Well, that's good," Tamara said. "Hire her to help you

with all your schoolwork, then when she's not helping you with schoolwork, she can do little things you need done around the station."

I shook off that thought. Did I really want to hang around a scrub like Valerie, even if she was working for me? I know some people hung around busters to make themselves look better. But I didn't need any help improving on the perfection that was Maya Morgan. Besides, I was the top of the food chain. I didn't need any scrubs bringing down my stock.

"I'll figure something out," I said.

Tamara shrugged as she pushed open the door to the building. "Well, let me know if you change your mind." She smiled as she held the door open for me. "As for now, let's go make history!"

Chapter 8

I had to pinch myself because I still couldn't believe that I was really sitting at the head—okay, maybe it was at the foot, but it felt like the head—of a huge conference-room table like I was the Queen of England. Tamara wasn't playing.

This was our third meeting in as many days. The first one—when Tamara had picked me up from school—had been to meet "my team," as they called it, and talk about the direction of the show. The second had been to shoot a bunch of promos and other stuff. All the stuff they were doing now made me realize how second-rate everything we'd done on *Miami Divas* had been. But I wasn't going to trip on the past—not when I had a future so bright it was sure to blind me!

My team was ready to move fast and had wasted no time going all out. They'd just finished filling me in on the plans for a total makeover. I didn't think it was possible to improve on perfection, but I was willing to see what they had, especially since they were talking about bringing in a new stylist and even a voice and elocution coach. I actually was shocked at how much they were putting into it. I was even more

shocked by the numbers on my contract. I was getting paid
three times what I'd been paid for *Miami Divas* and all those
perks we'd demanded? I had those and then some. My dad's
attorney had looked over everything and after going back
and forth on a few things, he'd been overjoyed at the final
contract. Me, I let him work out all that legal stuff. I just liked
the part about me being a superstar!

I wish I could drop out of school and just do this full
time, but since I'm too cute to be dumb, that wasn't an option. So, I went to school, did what I was supposed to, and got
up out of there. Tamara had the voice coach meet me during
my lunch so I didn't have to worry about seeing Sheridan
and everyone else. All of them—Sheridan, Shay, and Bali—
tried to create drama in the hallways and the one class we had
together. Even Chenoa had stopped speaking to me and she
wasn't even a *Diva*! But she was good friends with Evian
(that's a long story), so she went whichever way Evian was
going. Evian was the only one who didn't act fazed about
everything, but I didn't trust her either. She was one of those
sneaky chicks who would smile to your face while stabbing
you in your back with a butcher knife.

I was a little ticked at Sheridan, though. She was supposed
to be my girl, but now she was parading around, telling
everyone that she and Bryce were an item, which was jacked
up because we had a boy code that made talking to each
other's boyfriends or crushes a serious violation. I couldn't
believe that she'd gone there. But Kennedi had called Sheridan to tell her off about how she was acting toward me and
Sheridan had admitted that she was the one who told about
Kenny and she wasn't even apologetic about it (or about
throwing in the lie about Dave). So, not only had she lied on
me, but she moved in on my man without a second thought.
And Bryce's dumb behind had played right into her trap. I
suddenly found myself wondering if they'd been messing
around all along. But then I brushed the thought away. The

two of them could have each other. I had bigger fish to fry now.

"So, what do you think?" Ken, one of the producers of the show, asked me, snapping me out of my thoughts.

"It sounds great," I said. I didn't even know what he was talking about, but I didn't want them to think I wasn't paying attention. Tamara had asked me to adjust my attitude, so I was going to try—as long as these folks recognized who the real star was.

"Great. We'll do the Sylk exclusive, then the story with Justin Timberlake taking the girl to the prom, and then for the next show, we've already lined up Meagan Goode's one-on-one." Ken slid some papers across the table at me. "Here is some background on Meagan. You'll need to read over it just so you can be familiar with her."

I had to struggle to compose myself. I was actually about to interview Meagan Goode. Oh, it was about to be on.

"Here's some other background info on some more stories we're working on," Ken said, pushing more papers my way. "As I told you, we'll have a mixture of national entertainment news, but the bulk of our stuff will be local celebrity stuff."

I took the stack of papers. Good grief. They wanted me to read all this stuff?

"Just so you know, the promos are going to start running today," Tamara said, smiling in my direction. "I told you this was gonna move fast. Lincoln, let's show her the first commercial," she said, motioning to the guy sitting closest to the computer.

Lincoln turned toward the screen at the front of the room and pressed a remote control. The video started playing and my mouth dropped open. I looked even better than I thought—and I hadn't even thought that was possible. My outfit was on point, my hair was laid and I was a natural.

The narrator's voice filled the room. "Good gossip . . .

delicious buzz . . . no secret is safe at *Rumor Central*. And Maya Morgan is just the diva to dish the dirt." My picture popped up with me looking fierce in a Diane von Furstenberg plum wrap dress that dipped off the shoulder just a bit. My hair was seriously on point, with the lighting hitting my highlights in all the right places. Some high-tech music popped up as the narrator finished. "*Rumor Central*, the place to get all the celebrity dirt. Coming soon." Everyone smiled, pleased with the whole thing. A quick thought passed in my mind. We weren't based in Hollywood, where all the celebrities lived, so how was I supposed to bring the dirt on a regular basis?

Oh, who was I kidding? I might not have been speaking to my crew any longer, but we all were Miami's elite. That meant we knew some of everybody. So, finding dirt definitely wouldn't be a problem.

Chapter 9

I heard this comedian once say if you don't have at least ten haters, you ain't on your job. Well, I needed to be promoted because I was definitely excelling at my job!

But it was all good because all the shade Sheridan and the rest of them were throwing my way only motivated me even more. Like now, I ignored Bali's whispering (obviously about me) as I walked down the hall and I strutted with a fierceness reserved for the catwalk.

"Hey, Maya, wait up," Valerie called out, scurrying to catch up with me.

In the past, I would've ignored Valerie. Not that she'd done anything to me, but she just wasn't in my clique. But for these past two weeks, Valerie had been the only one not giving me grief. I'd actually gotten a B on my make-up exam but I hadn't yet taken the leap to make her my assistant.

"What's up, Valerie?"

"Nothing," she said, struggling to balance her books and keep them from falling. Seriously? Who even carried that many books to class? "I . . . I was just wondering if you'd given any thought to my suggestion. I'd still be willing to help you with your other classes. I've been on the honor roll since freshman year."

"Thank you," I found myself saying. "But . . ." I paused when I saw Sheridan and another girl approaching us, and something made me say, "I think I'll take you up on that offer. The station actually wanted me to get an assistant, so maybe you can help out there, too."

"Ohmygod, I so could do that!" Valerie squealed.

"I had actually been telling my producer how cool you'd been," I continued, "and I told her I could use someone like you on my team."

As expected, Sheridan stopped, trying to be nosy.

I pretended I didn't see her as I kept talking. "Matter of fact, I tape my first show tomorrow. Would you like to come on set and watch and then you can get right to work?"

While Sheridan didn't say anything, the girl standing next to her did. "I heard about your TV show. When does it start?"

"I tape the first show tomorrow," I said, smiling at her.

Sheridan rolled her eyes, but Valerie was too excited to notice.

"So is it true?" Valerie asked. "Are you really going to interview Meagan Goode?"

"Yep. And she's just the first of many celebrities. You won't believe the folks I have lined up. I can tell you, one of them is Nicki Minaj."

"You have got to be kidding me!" the girl standing with Sheridan shrieked. "I love Nicki. How you get that hookup?"

"I just got it like that," I said, shrugging.

"Wow, I want to be like you when I grow up," the girl laughed.

"Doesn't everybody?" I mumbled. Sheridan didn't bother to hide her disgust. I was eating her reaction up.

"So, I can really come on set?" Valerie quickly asked.

"Of course," I replied. "Just be at the studio by five. It's going to be so fab. They're so excited about my show and they're treating me like royalty."

"That's because you are, girl," Valerie said.

"Oh, give me a break," Sheridan said, storming off.

I laughed as we all watched her walk away. She was probably going to find some Pepto-Bismol because I had no doubt that she was sick!

"What's her problem?" Valerie asked.

I smiled, pulled out my sunglasses, and said, "The source of her envy is plain to see. Poor little Sheridan is hating because she can't be me. Smooches," I added as I runway-walked down the hall.

Chapter 10

My stomach was in knots. Today was the premiere of my show and I had an exclusive interview with Sylk, who was having a concert in town this weekend. I was still tripping that on my very first show I was actually going to be kickin' it with Sylk!

"Here you go," Valerie said, handing me a bottle of Fiji water and my notes for the show. I actually was grateful for Valerie's help. She'd shown up thirty minutes early, jumped right in, and already been a big help. "Do you need anything else?"

I shook my head. Oh, I could so get with this personal assistant thing. I needed to make sure Tamara would let me keep Valerie around, even after school ended. "I'm good. But if you can go look over my chemistry homework, that would be great," I said, flashing a smile her way. "It's in the purple folder in my messenger bag over there." I pointed in the corner. "If you see any blanks, can you be a doll and just fill it in, please?"

She nodded eagerly, then raced out. I hated to tell her, the whole thing would be blank because I hadn't so much as written my name. But that shouldn't be a problem. Schoolwork was Valerie's thing. Being fabulous was mine.

"All right. Let's get this party started," Tamara said, peeking her head into the small room they'd converted into my private dressing room (another one of my requests since I didn't want a whole bunch of people up in my personal space). "Do you have any questions?" she asked.

"Nope. Is Sylk here?" I knew rule number one of dealing with celebrities—don't act excited. So, I made a mental note to make sure I played it completely cool.

Tamara nodded. "She's in the Green Room." I tried to appear unfazed. I couldn't very well put Oprah out of her job if I was getting all excited over some celebrity.

Tamara came and stood in front of me. "Maya, I want you to know this is unprecedented," she began. "We're breaking new territory here. As you know, our station serves a young demographic. We may not be one of the big three, but we are definitely giving CW and Fox a run for their money."

I guess I looked confused because she smiled at me and said, "Our viewers are young. That's why we tapped you for this show. So we want you to be your young, vibrant self, but you've got to bring it."

"Oh, I have no trouble bringing it." I gave myself a once-over in the dressing room mirror. Then, satisfied, I turned back to face Tamara. "This is Maya Morgan's destiny. I was meant to be a star. Believe that." That was the truth because if I ever had any doubt, all I had to think about was the joy Bali and that whole crew would get in seeing me fail. Nope, failure wasn't an option.

"Okay, that's what I wanted to hear." She motioned for the door. "Let's do this!"

They just didn't know how ready I was to get started. I thought about this corny commercial I'd seen once. It said, *Today is the first day of the rest of your life.* That's how I felt today. I was about to go into a whole new stratosphere and I couldn't wait!

Chapter 11

I was still floating high as I glided down the hallway toward Tamara's corner office. She had sent me a text to come see her as soon as I got in today. She probably wanted to tell me what a fabulous job I'd done on the taping yesterday. "Tell me something I don't know," I mumbled to myself as I floated confidently down the hall. I had clicked like Sylk and I were best friends. I'd even gotten her to share some details about her new movie, which was supposed to be under wraps until next month, plus, I'd gotten her to address the rumors of her messing around with one of her co-stars. I was pretty proud of the first show and was sure that's what Tamara wanted to talk about.

Outside Tamara's office, I tapped on the door. "Hey there. You wanted to see me?"

"Yeah, come on in," Tamara said, waving me in.

I glanced over at Dexter, the senior producer on my show, who sat in front of Tamara's desk. "Hi, Dexter."

"Hey."

I felt an uneasy feeling in my stomach when he didn't really smile back at me.

"Please have a seat," Tamara said. The look on her face and the businesslike tone of her voice wiped the smile off my face as well.

Oh, no, I hoped she wasn't about to tell me they were having second thoughts. I eased into the chair in front of her desk, trying to figure out what in the world was going on.

"As you know, we thought you were a shoo-in for this job," Tamara began.

I felt my heartbeat speed up. *Thought? As in past tense?* "Oh my God. You think I suck?"

Both Dexter and Tamara let out small laughs. "No, we don't think you suck," Tamara said. "In fact, you're very good, a natural. And we think you have a very bright future ahead of you."

I relaxed a bit. Of course I didn't suck. Why in the world was I getting worked up?

Before I could say anything else, Tamara added, "The show, however, may suck just a little."

That shocked me. I thought the show was pretty good. I mean, it was Sylk after all.

Tamara paused like she was thinking. Finally she said, "The show is . . . how do I say this?"

"Boring," Dexter said, interrupting her.

"Not that we think *you're* boring," Tamara said, quickly jumping in. "We've just been assessing the first show all morning and it just lacks that umph. The Sylk interview was great, but we're not trying to be another *Entertainment Tonight*. We need to spice this thing up. We're hoping you can help bring some of that umph to the table."

Bring some umph? I didn't know what they expected me to do.

Dexter and Tamara exchanged uneasy glances before Tamara said, "You run in—" She paused. "I'm sorry, you *used* to run in some pretty well-known circles. I mean, not many teens can say they're friends with the Kardashians. There aren't many that get up close and personal with some of the hottest young celebrities."

"Yeah," I said, not sure where she was going. "That was part of what made us so popular. My clique was the real deal. But what does that have to do with anything? You want me to find some dirt on Miami celebrities?"

"Basically, and we thought you should start with your closest circle of friends. I mean, they are Miami's elite, so I'm sure you know some serious secrets."

I frowned. "Yeah, but those are my friends."

"Were," Tamara reminded me.

"And therefore, you shouldn't have any problem dishing dirt on them," Dexter added.

Tamara smiled knowingly. "I mean, that is what our show introduction says . . . that you'll be dishing dirt."

"So you really want me to dish dirt *on my friends*?"

Tamara didn't blink as she replied. "Which friend would you be referring to? Sheridan, the one that stole your boyfriend, or Shay, the one that jumped you in the hall?"

That definitely shut me up. I couldn't believe she was using information I'd shared with her in confidence.

"Look, this isn't personal," Tamara said, drumming her fingers on her desk. "This is business and if we want this show to be a success, we've got to come out of the box hard."

"Okay, well, what do you want me to do?" For the first time since I took this job, I was worried about it succeeding. The way they were talking, we were doomed before we even really started.

"I'm sure there are some salacious rumors or some celebrity gossip that you can dig up, something that you can give us about your in crowd," Tamara continued.

"I can't do that," I slowly said. It's not that I cared two cents about those busters, but the last thing I wanted to be was some kind of snitch. I'd thought about it. I mean, they'd made me so mad, that I couldn't believe I was even second-guessing selling them out.

"Are you in the in crowd anymore?" Tamara asked bluntly.

"Don't get it twisted. First of all, the Miami Divas weren't my only friends. I still roll with the in crowd. In fact, I *am* the in crowd."

"No, you're on the outside looking in," Tamara said. "At least at Miami High. Here's a way for you to have the last laugh."

I hesitated, then finally said, "I just don't . . ."

"I'm sorry. If you can't do it . . ." Tamara paused and looked at Dexter, who finished her sentence.

"Maybe Sheridan won't have any problems dishing dirt. Isn't she the daughter of that superstar singer? Maybe she'd do it," Dexter said, like he was dismissing me or something.

I was dumbfounded by his comment. "You'd give my job to Sheridan?"

"Of course we wouldn't *want* to do that, but I bet Sheridan would have no shame in dishing dirt," Tamara said. I couldn't believe she was playing me like that. I thought we were cool.

"I'm sure she wouldn't," Dexter threw in for good measure. "Especially your dirt."

I'm sure they were trying to punk me, but honestly, it was working. I'd never live it down if they fired me and gave my job to Sheridan.

Tamara continued talking. "So, the question is do you want Sheridan to get the guy *and* your job?" Tamara asked. I know she could tell they were getting to me.

Of course not, I thought. Even though I didn't say anything, she must've read the look on my face because she said, "Then I suggest you go home and get to digging in the back of your memory and come up with some juicy gossip."

I stood for a moment, trying to figure out my next move. I know we were the who's who of Miami, but did people really want to know our dirt like that? I thought about shows like TMZ and blogs like MediaTakeout and Bossip. Of course they did.

"I got it. You want dirt, I'll give you dirt." I sighed. "Do I need to work today?" I finally asked.

"No, because unless you come up with something, there's no work to be done," Dexter spoke matter-of-factly.

I felt sick in the pit of my stomach. I couldn't believe this. I was really going to be a snitch? Could I really sell out my friends? Images of this last month flashed before my eyes. I pictured my fight with Shay, all the hate I was getting at school. Then I thought about Sheridan and Bryce at the homecoming dance and I had my answer. Not only could I do this, I would take great pleasure in doing it.

Chapter 12

I couldn't believe I was hanging out with Valerie Elgin. On the misfit scale, she was definitely nearing a ten. Honestly, I wondered how she even could stand to look at herself in the mirror. From her drab, stringy hair, which she always wore pulled back into a raggedy ponytail to her too-big clothes hanging from her body, she was so far from fab, it made my skin crawl. But then, when I thought about the other geeks she hung out with—another nerdy girl named Jennifer and this guy named Eugene who needed to star in his own *Extreme Dork* show.

Looking at Valerie now, she probably would be pretty if she got rid of those Coke-bottle glasses, colored her hair, and got a decent wardrobe.

"So, do you get it?" Valerie asked. She had been spending the last hour at my house trying to help me get ready for yet another stupid calculus test. Like, who would ever use calculus again in life?

"I guess," I said. "Although I can't for the life of me understand why I have to know this stupid stuff."

Valerie shrugged. "It's not that bad if you give it a chance. I really like it. Sometimes I do calculus just for fun."

Calculus for fun? Nerd strike number two.

"So, just review the notecards I made." She pointed to the stack of cards that I knew I wasn't about to pick up. I didn't say anything else as we gathered up our stuff and headed downstairs.

"You want something to drink?" I asked when we made it into our theater room.

"If you don't mind," Valerie replied.

I yelled for Sui, our maid, who came running into the room. "Yes, Miss Morgan?" she said.

"Hey, Sui, can you make me and my friend some lemonade and bring it to the theater room?"

Sui nodded and disappeared back in the kitchen. I turned to see Valerie with a stupid grin on her face.

"What's your problem?" I asked.

"Nothing," she said, still smiling, *"friend."*

Oh, good grief, she was really cheesing over me calling her a friend. Truthfully, it had just slipped out, but I shrugged it off. Between that and me inviting her to hang out a minute—don't ask me why I'd done that—Valerie was probably ready to get matching BFF necklaces made.

"So, do you mind if I ask why you don't hang with your old friends from the show anymore?" Valerie asked once we were settled in the den and I'd turned on the TV.

I knew Valerie had been dying to ask me that since I'd let her into my world. At first, I thought about telling her some elaborate lie, but I was about to blow up and I didn't really care if she knew. Besides, it was all over school that we were no longer friends, and most people knew it was because of my show. I just hadn't told anyone the details.

"Their true colors showed after I got my own show. I couldn't take the hate," I said.

She shook her head. "That's so lame. These privileged

kids don't know how good they have it. It's not even necessary to hate on other people."

"Yeah, you're right," I said, telling myself that she obviously couldn't be talking about me. Sui brought our lemonade and Valerie and I sat and talked about one of the rap videos on TV, as well as a bunch of other stuff. I was trippin' over how mad cool Valerie had turned out to be when she was talking about something other than school.

"Well, it's getting late," Valerie said after about an hour. "I'd better get going."

We stood and I walked her to the back, where I'd had her park. My mom would've had a stroke if she had come home and seen Valerie's raggedy Toyota Prius parked in front of our house.

"Dang, where are my keys?" Valerie said, patting her pockets.

I looked around and spotted them on a table by the door. "Is this them?" I asked, picking up the set of keys.

"Yep," she said, holding her hands out.

A picture dangling on the end caught my eye. It was a photo of a gray-haired couple in the wackest clothes I'd ever seen. They wore matching flowered shirts with gigantic collars. "Who is this?" I asked. "Are these your grandparents?" Talk about lame. I loved my grandparents, but I wouldn't be caught dead carrying a picture of them around on my keychain.

She quickly snatched the keys. "No, those are my parents," she said defensively.

"Dang, they're old," I frowned. "What, did they have you when they were like in their fifties or something?"

"No." She looked down at the picture, then back up at me. Her eyes looked all sad as she added, "My parents are good people. They're just old, but they mean the world to me."

Dang, I thought. Talk about bringing somebody down. I

started to say something else, but then decided I didn't really want to know. I needed to go get my beauty rest for tomorrow, plus I had to do research for tomorrow's show, so Valerie's sob story about her parents would have to wait for another day.

Chapter 13

Tamara was blowing up my phone. I knew it was because it had been three days and she was expecting some juicy dirt from me, but so far, I hadn't come up with anything major and I was supposed to report to work tomorrow. I had one big story and a few other things I was working on, but I didn't know if it was going to be juicy enough for them. Word was that our vice-principal used to be a man, but I quickly put that into the "who really cares" file. Besides, Tamara had said she wanted more celebrity dirt.

"Hey, Maya, what's up?" my friend Angie said, approaching me. She was with some of her fellow cheerleaders and they all just looked at me without speaking. I didn't sweat it though because I knew they were just some jealous trolls. But I was hot over the fact that Chenoa, who I thought was cool with me, turned her nose up and walked off. Trick. With the things I knew about her, she might want to check that stank attitude.

I inhaled, deciding not to let her get to me. "Hey, Angie," I said, not bothering to speak to the others.

"Did you get Ms. Watson's paper done?" she asked as we made our way inside the building.

"Girl, please," I said, rolling my eyes. "Don't even get me started. I am so far behind."

"I heard you got that nerd, Valerie, to help you. Is she tutoring you?" Angie asked.

I couldn't tell if she was being nosey or what, but she had her nose turned up like she was disgusted.

"She isn't tutoring me. Just with my schedule, I needed an assistant," I replied. I didn't need anyone knowing that I was failing my classes.

"Oh, I'm not trippin'," she added. "Shoot, I had to get her buster friend, Jennifer, to tutor me." Angie turned to one of the other cheerleaders who had hung back waiting on her. "At least these ratchet scholarship students are good for something," she laughed as they high-fived each other.

I laughed with her. The scholarship kids at our school got a serious bad rap. Most of them came from underprivileged families and families that couldn't afford the school. Personally, I felt like if you couldn't afford Miami High, you needed to take your butt to the disgusting public school down the street.

Chenoa was the only one not laughing. She looked back at Angie and said, "Come on, Angie. We need to get to the gym or Mrs. Burkett is gonna have a stroke."

"Bye, girl," Angie said, darting off down the hall.

I waved bye and had just made it to my locker, when I spotted Bryce standing over Sheridan. It looked like they were arguing, but as soon as she spotted me, she threw her arms around his neck and started kissing him to the point that someone yelled for them to "get a room."

It felt like someone had punched me in my stomach and if half the hallway hadn't been staring at me, I would've turned around and gone the other way. But since they were, I kept strutting like I wasn't fazed.

"Excuse me," I said, pointing to my locker, which they were leaned up against. I knew I should've moved my locker away from Sheridan when we first fell out. "Can I get in my locker, please?"

Bryce saw me and looked super embarrassed, but Sheridan just smirked. "My bad, got a little caught up." She giggled and I wanted to punch her in her teeth.

Bryce looked apologetic, but remained quiet. I so couldn't stand either of them. She was a backstabbing troll and he was so dumb he couldn't see she was playing him just to get back at me.

I ignored her as I unlocked my locker and tossed one book in, then pulled another one out.

"So, Maya, did you get a date to the homecoming dance?" she asked, wrapping her arm around Bryce's waist.

"Bi—" I caught myself before I went off. I was not about to let her take me there. I took a deep breath, then smiled as I closed my locker. I ran my eyes up and down her body, didn't say a word, then laughed as I walked off. I could feel her eyes piercing my back.

"That is so tight how you played her," Valerie said, catching up with me as I rounded the corner. "Everybody saw it. I hate how Sheridan acts so high and mighty." Valerie leaned in. "If she knew the truth, she might think twice about treating people like crap."

That made me stop in my tracks. "What truth?" I asked. Sheridan and I had been super tight, so I couldn't imagine there was something about her that I didn't know.

Valerie leaned back and smiled. "I know something about Miss Sheridan's superstar mother, the fabulous Glenda Matthews."

"What?" I asked, eager to hear any dirt about Sheridan's mom. Glenda Matthews was one of the hottest stars in Hollywood. She had like a million Grammys, had had several big-time movie roles, and was always traveling overseas or staying at their Los Angeles home, which is why Sheridan ran out of control. They were from Miami and the plan had been that her family was supposed to be watching her, but they took Ms. Matthews's money and left Sheridan to fend for herself. And since Sheridan liked her freedom, her mom didn't even know.

"Well," Valerie began, "I heard it through the grapevine that Glenda Matthews had a kid and gave her up for adoption for a movie role because she didn't want to tarnish her image." Valerie stood back, I guess to take in my shock. And I was definitely shocked.

"Are you serious?"

"Yep," Valerie said confidently.

"How do you know that? I've been friends with Sheridan for years and I've never heard that." That had to be some kind of mistake. I couldn't stand her now, but Sheridan and I used to share everything and I can't believe she would know something like that and not tell me.

"Sheridan didn't tell because Sheridan doesn't know herself."

I was definitely all ears now. "Get out of here. How do you know this?"

Valerie smiled mischievously. "You know you guys aren't the only ones that hear gossip."

"What do you mean?"

She pulled me to the side and lowered her voice. "Well, I've got a little gossip of my own." She looked around to make sure no one was listening. "My friend Jennifer's mother works at an adoption agency," Valerie whispered. "She swore me to secrecy because her mother could lose her job, but apparently, Miss Glenda Matthews got knocked up right before her role in that Cleopatra movie, you know the one that put her on the map?"

Of course I knew about that one. Everyone did. I also knew that role had launched Ms. Matthews's career and was the one that had put Sheridan's mom on the map. She had been an unknown singer before that and it had ended up earning her an Academy Award and a Grammy.

"Well," Valerie continued, "Ms. Glenda Matthews wasn't about to let anything stand in the way of that role, including the fact that she was seven months pregnant."

"How the heck did she hide that?"

Valerie shrugged. "I have no idea. But she did. Didn't tell a soul, then ditched her kid and kept it moving."

I leaned back against the wall, dumbfounded. "Wow. Just wow." I took in her words. "But, wait a minute. If she didn't tell anyone, how do people know?"

"Well, she put the kid up for adoption and that's how Jennifer's mom found out. She was so disgusted when she saw Glenda win an Academy Award a few years ago, she broke down and told her husband and Jenn overheard her."

"I just can't believe it. This is crazy."

"Tell me about it. So, like I said, she's trying to act like she's all that. If only she knew." Valerie laughed, then looked at her watch. "Let me get to class. I'll see you at the studio."

I waved good-bye and stood processing everything.

We'd been pretty crappy to Valerie and her friends over the years. Even when I worked with Valerie on the school newspaper, I didn't talk to her unless I had to. So, I was shocked that Valerie hadn't already let that secret loose. But I did know one thing, Sheridan might not have known about her illegitimate brother or sister, but if I had anything to do with it, it was just a matter of time before she did know and that would be the ultimate payback.

Chapter 14

I was decked out in my fly Burberry silk wrap dress and four-inch Manolos. My hair was hooked up and my makeup was tight. The producers of *Rumor Central* wanted scandal and I was definitely about to give it to them. All thanks to a little secret I knew about Miss Evian Javid. I used her phone one day and saw a text message from one of her "girls." Not girls the way Kennedi and Lauren were my girls, but like "they-work-for-me" girls.

I had been fascinated when Evian finally confessed to her little side hustle, because everyone thought she was so prim and proper, but Evian was a straight businesswoman. She was actually the one who ran the escort service. She'd gotten Chenoa on board, and she had been surprised at how much money she'd earned and how fast. Chenoa had quickly recruited some more girls. I'd been stunned at how they'd been able to keep it under wraps. It wasn't until Chenoa acted so stank in the hallway the other day, that it even dawned on me that this was exactly the type of story Tamara and Dexter wanted.I probably should've been nervous because I knew today's show was about to take my beef with the former *Miami Divas* to a whole other level. But Maya Morgan was

destined for stardom and if this was how I had to get it, then
so be it.

The makeup artist patted some of the shine off my nose,
then gave me a reassuring look as if to say, *You got this*.

I smiled. I knew I did, but I felt more nervous today than
I had on the first show. Maybe because I knew that I was
about to reach the point of no return. Naturally, the producers had been thrilled about the cheerleader story. The research team had dived in and in less than twenty-four hours
had confirmed enough for us to run with. We weren't like
the real shows that had to confirm and validate everything.
We just needed enough to keep us from getting sued. They
were having a harder time confirming details about Ms.
Matthews (yes, I had run straight to the producers and shared
that story. *And?*) so that story had to wait. Still, I had no doubt
that they'd get enough. But for now, it was all about the
cheerleaders.

I wasn't completely stupid though. Evian's family was
ruthless so I wasn't going to tie her to the ring, but I was
going to expose it and if she started tripping with me, I
would quickly remind her that if anything, she needed to be
thanking me for keeping her name out of it. I had just
planned to pretend the station was on to the story anyway.

I waited for the director to give me my cue to go live.
And within minutes, he was counting me down.

"And five, four, three, two, one . . ." The director waved
for me to start.

And start I did.

"Hey, hey, hey, what's up? Welcome to *Rumor Central*,
where we dish the dirt on the celebs you love," I began.
"You'll want to make sure you don't change that channel because have we got some dirt for you. It involves some Miami
cheerleaders who are giving new meaning to the phrase
'we've got spirit.' They have spirit, yes they do. Just ask the
clients of their private escort ring. That's right, the ladies of

one Miami cheerleading squad are known for their antics on the field, but it's off the field that they are making their biggest moves."

I knew that it wouldn't be difficult to figure out which school it was. We'd blurred the cheerleaders' faces, but they still had on their maroon and white uniforms. I knew this story would make the school look bad, but Tamara wanted scandal and I had to deliver.

"This award-winning cheer squad is great at getting the fans riled up, but they're even better at reining the men in," I continued. The video cut to another picture of three cheerleaders wearing sexy little outfits.

"That's right, rumor has it that these seventeen-year-olds are playing with the big girls." I leaned in. "But we're not ones to gossip, so you didn't hear it from us. Stay with us. We'll have all the scandalicious details after the break."

After the commercial, I continued spilling the dirt, tossed to another commercial break, then finished out the show.

I'd barely taken my mic off when Dexter came racing on to the set. "That's what I'm talking about! That's what we need! Maya, that show was fiyah!"

I laughed at his attempt at using slang.

"Oh, I guarantee you that this story will be in all the papers tomorrow and that's just what we want," he continued, his excitement overtaking him. "We just want to be able to light a fire and it can take off from there."

He kissed me on the cheek and said, "You're the best ever," before darting off.

"Wow," Valerie said, easing up next to me. "I knew you were planning to go hard, but I didn't know you were going to like that."

Per Tamara's request, I'd kept the major gossip stories we were working on under wraps. Tamara didn't want me telling anyone because she didn't want anything getting out ahead of time, so Valerie didn't have a clue what stories I was working on.

"Yeah, well, just doing my job," I said casually.

I looked down at my cell phone and the words in all caps filled the screen.

YOU LOW-DOWN DIRTY SNAKE!!!

It came from Evian's phone.

YOU ARE SO GOIN TO B SORRY!!

Now this chick was threatening me? I angrily punched in a reply.

B glad I didn't tell who the queen of the ring is. B/c we both know I could have.

U r so goin' to regret this, she typed back.

And if I do, u & ur little ring will regret it a whole lot more. No one knows ur name . . . yet. F-w/me & they will.

I tried to keep it classy, but I needed to let Evian know I would not be intimidated. Not now, not ever.

Chapter 15

I'd known that people weren't going to be happy about my show, but I never expected this type of reception. As I made my way down the hallway, members of the drill team gave me the evil eye and I swear, if looks could kill . . .

"Trifling witch," someone said as I passed.

I heard someone else mutter another derogatory word, but one of the things I had learned from my dad was to never let them see you sweat and I wasn't about to give these busters the satisfaction.

I heard someone yell, "There she is!"

Within minutes, the head cheerleader, Chenoa, and other members of the cheerleading squad came stomping my way.

"You are so f-ing foul," Chenoa spat. She stepped in my face and I swear, it took everything in my power not to run because she looked like she was about to haul off and knock the mess out of me. I wasn't a fighter, but I felt like I could hold my own if I had to. I just wasn't trying to go there ever again.

"I can't believe you ran that story," Chenoa said, her voice filled with anger.

"It's the truth." I shrugged. "That's what I do, get to the truth."

"Your stupid show is called *Rumor Central,*" she screamed. "You don't know what the truth is!"

"Yeah, it's just a bunch of gossip and trash," one of the other cheerleaders said.

"Then, if it's not true, why are you so worked up?" I calmly said.

Chenoa's eyes actually watered up as she took a different tone. "I thought that you were my girl."

I almost busted out laughing. "*Your girl?* You hadn't had two words to say to me in the last three weeks. Now, all of a sudden, I'm your girl? Please," I said, opening my locker, throwing in my books, and slamming the door shut. I couldn't believe her nerve.

"How could you do this?" Evian said, stepping up and whispering in my ear. She had eased up behind the cheerleaders and they'd parted like she was some kind of royalty.

I ignored her.

"You know you're messing with the wrong people," she warned.

I shrugged nonchalantly, even though her icy tone sent shivers up my spine.

"I'm just doing my job. If you have a beef, take it up with the station," I said.

Chenoa wagged her finger. I hadn't even realized she'd stepped on the other side of me. They were on both sides of me like a sandwich. "Oh, you'd better believe my dad already has his attorney on it. You and your funky show are about to go down."

I stared straight at her. "And I'm sure that you had to play up the innocent role with Daddy. But we all know the truth and if I were you, I wouldn't want Daddy to go digging around because he might just turn up some stuff he doesn't want to know."

That made her stop. Obviously, she hadn't thought about that.

Evian must've decided she was going to try and reason with me because she stepped toward me, but this time, she didn't have as much of an attitude. "Do you have any idea what kind of trouble they are in?" she asked.

"Yeah, Mr. Carvin has already ordered us to his office at lunchtime," Chenoa threw in. She, on the other hand, still had major attitude.

"Not my problem," I said. I wasn't cocky or anything, but they needed to understand that I was just doing my job. Too bad, so sad if they couldn't understand that.

The tallest cheerleader on the squad, Zenobia, took a step toward me. "I ought to knock the mess out of you," she said.

I didn't let my fear show on my face as I said, "Then do it and make sure your daddy's attorney is on standby when I sue you because I don't fight. I sue."

"Zenobia, I know you are not about to resort to violence in my hallway," a booming voice interrupted us.

Me and Zenobia's Amazon-looking self faced off, ignoring the principal who then stepped in between us.

Mr. Carvin looked directly at me. "And you, I think you have bigger problems," he said. "You don't need to add violence to your list." He turned to the other cheerleaders. "In my office, *now*. All of you," he said, motioning toward the cheerleaders. But before he left, he made sure to shoot me the evil eye. "And Miss Morgan, I need to see you after school as well."

"But I have to work," I protested.

"That wasn't a request," he said, as he turned and walked away.

"If I were you, I'd watch my back," Zenobia said, as she passed me, bumping my shoulder.

Whatever. I wasn't going to lose any sleep over them.

The one thing I did know is that they covered their tracks well and if they didn't, each of their daddies had more than enough money to get them out of trouble.

"You all right?" I hadn't even realized Valerie was beside me the whole time. I found myself wondering if she would have had my back or if she would have run for cover if something had gone down. Judging from the fear in her face, ol' girl would've definitely jetted.

"I'm cool. I knew I was going to get some backlash."

"They're just hating," Valerie said, walking along beside me. "They take great pleasure in making life miserable for the rest of us and they can't take their own medicine."

"I guess they can't. It's just that—"

Before I could finish, she nudged me. "Look who's coming your way."

I looked up and Bryce was walking up with Mike, another one of his teammates. They were walking directly toward us, so there was no pretending that I didn't see them.

"Yo, that's jacked up what you did, girl," Mike said. But the smile on his face told me he actually wasn't upset with me. "But I'm not even gonna lie, you got the whole school buzzing, I tell you that much."

"Then I guess I'm doing my job," I said confidently, not bothering to acknowledge Bryce.

Mike grinned. "So is it true that you have an interview with Nicki Minaj?"

I smiled back. They'd teased that during last night's show with a whole "Nicki's got a secret" campaign. "Yeah, I'm gonna interview her on the red carpet. She'll share her secret, then I'm doing a backstage special."

"For real?" Mike said, excitedly. "What a brother gotta do to get the hook-up?"

I couldn't help it. I noticed Bryce shift uncomfortably and I found myself flirting. "A brother gotta know the right thing to do," I said, squeezing his cheek. Any other time, he would've completely grossed me out. But just the thought of sticking it to Bryce made me push on.

I took his cell phone out of his hand and punched my phone number in. "Call me and I'll hook you up. Maybe you can come for the taping and meet Nicki in person."

"For real?" he asked in excitement.

I nodded, smiling.

"Wow. Can I bring a friend?" he asked.

I side-eyed Bryce. "It all depends on who that friend is," I said, not cracking a smile as I walked off.

I wondered if Bryce's eyes were on me as I sashayed down the hall. But I didn't need to wonder. I was rocking a new Valentino skirt that was hugging me in all the right places. My strappy wedges showed off my athletic calves. Yeah, I knew his eyes were on me. And I knew watching me walk away had to have him sick. And that was just the way I liked it.

Chapter 16

I stared at the paper in my hand, a huge smile plastered across my face. It wasn't like I hadn't seen this much money before. Shoot, I could spend that in a day, but there was something about knowing I'd earned this all on my own that really felt good.

"Maya, honey, why are you standing in the middle of the kitchen?" my mom joked as she walked in the room. My dad was standing right behind her. They looked like they'd just come in from playing tennis—something they both loved doing together. "Are you about to make dinner?" my mom asked.

"No, just checking out my hard work," I replied.

She looked around the kitchen. "Oh my. You cleaned up the kitchen?"

"Get real, Mom," I said. "I'm talking about this. Bam." I put the check for five thousand dollars down on the counter.

My mother eyed the check. "What's this?" she said picking it up.

"My paycheck," I sang. My mom smiled.

My dad was ecstatic. "Maya, I am so incredibly proud of you," he said, taking the check from my mom.

"Doesn't it feel good to earn your own money?" he asked.

I flashed a smile. "It feels better spending yours." I took the check from him, folded it, and dropped it in my purse. "But it does feel good earning my own."

"Let's go shopping," my mom said. "You know it's not a whole lot that we can do with five grand, but maybe we can go to the spa and stock up on beauty supplies."

My dad narrowed his eyes at my mom. "Liza, don't teach the child to spend money before she even gets it. I put you two on a budget and things need to stay that way."

"This is ridiculous. So now, I'm like some teen that has to ask daddy for permission to shop," my mom shot back.

"You and your daughter's shopping is out of control! Your American Express bill last month was thirty-four-thousand dollars!"

"*And*?"

"Liza, I can't do this with you now," he said, picking up the mail and sifting through it, all but dismissing her.

I couldn't do it either. I was so not in the mood for their fights. "I'm going to my room. I have to get ready for my show tomorrow."

"Maya," my dad called out, stopping me just before I reached the bottom of the staircase. "Just know that I—" He looked at my mom. "We both are extremely proud of you."

I was proud of myself as well, so much so that the fact that they'd taken something I'd done and made it all about them didn't bother me.

I made my way back up the stairs and into my room. I needed to call Kennedi and share my joy at my news of such a huge paycheck, which included my salary, and a Red Carpet bonus. Her mom was always on her case about money, even though they had plenty of it. So, she would definitely appreciate the fact that I had my own money. I wanted to tell somebody other than my parents. I mean, Valerie and I were cool, but she was actually working for free so what would I look like rubbing my paycheck in her face?

I pulled my check back out, fell back over my bed, and dialed Kennedi's number. It went to her voicemail after three rings.

"Hey, Ken, it's me. Call me when you can. Got something I want to tell you," I said. I hung up the phone and debated calling Lauren, but since I knew her parents had cut her off financially, the last thing I wanted was to be waving some money in her face. I scrolled through my contact list. I smiled when I saw my cousins' names. "You could always call Nina and Tina," I laughed to myself. As if. I would never be that desperate. They were only a year behind me, but we had absolutely nothing in common. As cool as Nina and Tina could be at family get togethers, I wasn't trying to hang with them outside of that.

I spotted Sheridan and Evian's names in the favorites section of my contact list. For the first time, I actually found myself missing my girls. But knowing Sheridan's jealous behind, she probably would've just reminded me how her purse cost eight thousand dollars.

"Forget them," I mumbled, holding my check up and admiring it. "I don't need anything but this."

After a couple of minutes, I finally got up and dropped the check back in my purse.

I dropped down on my bed, flipped the TV on, and started flipping channels. I stopped on Channel 4, and my mouth dropped open as the news anchor broadcast a story about P. Diddy's house being broken into and vandalized.

"Police in South Miami are searching for a band of criminals that are going around and breaking into celebrity homes. Their latest victim is rap mogul P. Diddy, who had his summer home vandalized. Authorities are unsure how the crooks get past the security system, but more than eleven homes have been hit in the Miami–Dade area. And authorities think they may be all tied together."

"I'll tell you how they're getting past those systems," I mumbled. "Blake's father owns one of the biggest security firms in the country."

I laughed when I thought about the Bling Ring as Bali called them. I actually thought they'd chilled out, but I guess they were at it again.

Suddenly, it was like a light bulb went off and I jumped up and raced to my closet and grabbed a box off the top shelf. I dumped the contents on my bed, then smiled when I felt the small digital tape. I couldn't believe I'd forgotten about this. But me seeing this news report and remembering this, oh yeah, that was karma, baby, and I was ready to deliver yet another payback.

Chapter 17

It was going to be hard to top the cheerleading scandal, but I had no doubt that I had delivered.

"So, this is real?" Dexter asked, looking at me in disbelief as he paused the video playing on the big screen at the front of the room.

I nodded, pushing away that gnawing feeling inside my stomach.

Bali was going to go off when he found out what I'd done. I quickly pushed that thought aside. Bali's feelings were no longer my concern.

"It's as real as it gets," I added.

Tamara smiled slyly. "What did I tell you? Was she the girl to deliver, or what?"

Dexter looked like he was drooling. "Boy, was she ever." He smiled at Tamara. "Your idea to get someone on the inside of that glitzy teen world was right on target." He turned back to me. "This is exactly the kind of stuff I'm talking about. This is the kind of stuff we need to get people talking."

Ken, the assistant producer, leaned in and looked closer at the screen. "Now, tell me again who these people are."

I sighed heavily. I'd explained this to everyone three times already, but I started again since Ken had walked in on the tail end of the video.

"Okay, that is Amanda Hall," I said, pointing to the tall blonde in the first video. "She's Jazzy J's daughter."

"Like, *the* Jazzy J," Ken asked, "as in the multimillion-dollar rapper-producer, Jazzy J?"

"The one and only," I said, nodding before pointing to the other two people in the video. "And that's Sabrina Fulton, daughter of Clyde Fulton, the real estate mogul, and Blake Lewis, Jr."

Ken swung his head around. "Any relation to Blake Lewis, Sr., of Lewis Security Systems?"

Tamara, Dexter, and I all smiled. "Yep, you're looking at the son of Mr. Invincible Security himself," Dexter said, referring to the well-known commercial Blake's family ran about how foolproof their security systems were.

"Well, lean me over and spank me silly," Ken exclaimed. I had no idea what that corny mess meant, but I guessed, from the way he was cheesing so hard, it meant he was super excited.

"I just can't believe they are really and truly breaking into a mansion, and filming it?" Dexter said, still stunned.

When he said it like that it sounded pretty stupid, but when Bali had first filled us in on the Bling Ring, we'd all thought it was kind of cool. Bali and Sabrina were best friends, so that's how I knew about it. Bali had left the tape at my house after we watched it one day. They kept the Bling Ring under wraps, but those who did know about it actually thought it was kinda cool that they could get in and out without getting caught.

"Yeah, that's what they do," I said. "They go in, steal stuff, and then sell it on the black market."

"Why?" Tamara asked. "It's not like any of them don't have the means to buy this stuff."

"It's the thrill of it all," I replied. "Look," I felt compelled to add, "I want to get this story out there, but is there a way that we can do it without anyone going to jail?" I couldn't believe I was coming to their defense, but while I couldn't stand those trolls, I wasn't trying to see anyone get locked up, especially because I'd snitched.

"I guess we can blur their faces," Tamara said, looking at Dexter. "Right?"

He nodded, but I could tell he really didn't want to do it. It was all about the drama at *Rumor Central* and showing their faces would definitely bring the drama.

"Then it's all set," Tamara said. " 'The Bling Ring exposed' will be the subject of our next *Rumor Central*." She turned to me. "And Maya, might I add—good work. We needed you to deliver and you definitely did. I can't wait to see what you come up with."

I took in her praises, actually proud of myself for remembering the tape. But what I needed to know now was how in the world was I going to top that?

Chapter 18

My mind was still churning for the next big story as I made my way inside the house. My crew got into a lot of stuff over the years, but I'd been racking my brain trying to figure out what was "ratings worthy" and so far, I was coming up empty.

I'd barely opened the door leading into the kitchen. When my dad appeared, he looked frazzled.

"Maya, what in the world is going on? I got a call from Chenoa Montgomery's dad and he's furious. He said something about your show and spreading gossip. He's threatening to sue you."

I sighed. I should've known this was coming. "It's not gossip, Daddy," I said, walking in and dropping my keys and purse on the counter.

"Well, the show is called *Rumor Central*, so obviously it's some kind of gossip," he replied. For my dad to be so ruthless in the boardroom, I couldn't understand why he was getting all worked up.

I turned to him and tried to put on my reassuring face. "We still verify the stuff. Besides, I didn't give any of their names," I protested. The legal department had briefed me on how to address the upset people, so I was ready for any questions my dad threw at me. "So, I'm not sure why everyone's tripping."

"Mr. Montgomery said you said cheerleaders from a local high school and you showed the uniforms. That's not too hard to figure out."

"It's not my fault they want to be high-class call girls."

My dad paced back and forth, a habit he had when he was nervous. "Well, I don't like this. I thought this show was a good idea, but now this sounds like more trouble than it's worth."

I knew I needed to go into defensive mode. I had to get my parents' permission to do the show since I was under eighteen, and I didn't need either one of them tripping with me. "Look, Dad. You told me yourself that the people who succeed at their job almost always do it at the expense of someone else. What did you call it? Survival of the fittest?"

I could tell he was feeling the fact that I actually recited one of his work mottos.

"I am proud of you and the fact that you've found work that you enjoy," my father stated. "I just wish you could have found something more, I don't know, honest. Maybe you should rethink this job."

Oh, now he was for real tripping.

"What? Think about it, Dad. Your seventeen-year-old daughter is making more than half the people in this world who have full-time jobs."

That brought a small smile to his face. If anything could put stuff into perspective for my dad, it was money. "You are right about that."

I knew I had him, I just needed to keep at it, so I could bring him over to my side.

"Dad, you know I've always dreamed of being a journalist." That was the truth. I actually was one of the few kids who had known what she wanted to be since middle school. My first choice was to not work at all, but if I did have to work, I wanted to be an entertainment reporter.

"But this isn't really journalism," he replied.

"You know I wanted to be on TV. And this is perfect. How many seventeen-year-olds in this country do you know that have their own show?"

He smiled again. "That's because you're a Morgan."

As president of a multimillion-dollar company, my dad thrived on money, power and respect. Like my mother, I'd learned long ago that pumping him up was the best way to get whatever I wanted.

"And Morgans play to win, give our best, strive for the best and accept nothing but the best—at all times—and by any means necessary," I said with confidence.

He laughed. "That's my girl."

"You taught me well."

He sighed, then picked up his briefcase, which meant that we were done discussing this. "Okay, just watch yourself. I don't want you getting into any trouble."

"Relax, Dad. The station's legal team is on top of everything. I mean, if anyone is going to sue anyone, they'll sue the station. They can't sue me."

He turned to me. "Just be careful. Chenoa's dad sounded pretty angry."

I folded my arms across my chest and rolled my eyes. Mr. Montgomery probably thought his daughter was some sweet little princess. If only he knew. "That's because he doesn't want to face what his daughter really is," I said.

"I'm just grateful that you're not caught up in anything like that."

"And I never would be."

That seemed to pacify him and he kissed me on the top of the head as he headed out the door.

I had to give myself props. I was famous (well, even more famous), making money, and now my daddy was firmly on my side. Life didn't get any better than this.

Chapter 19

"And five, four, three, two . . ." The director, Manny, waved his finger to give me the cue to begin. I was ready. For the show and the aftermath once this story aired.

The theme music wound down and I began talking. "Hello and welcome to *Rumor Central*, where we dish the dirt on the celebrities you love. Boy, have we got a good one for you today. What do Diddy, Paris, and Shaq all have in common? No, it's not that they make their homes in Miami. It's that all those homes have been hit by the notorious Bling Ring. You've probably heard the stories. Police haven't been able to catch the crafty crooks, but *Rumor Central* has managed to track down some exclusive details," I said with a slight smile. "That's right. *Rumor Central* has the scoop, the lowdown, the nitty-gritty, the 411 on who's behind the Bling Ring. And you won't believe your ears . . . or your eyes. Stay tuned."

I could see Dexter in the control room giddy with excitement. The stylist rushed over and adjusted my David Yurman necklace, then brushed a strand of hair out of my face. Valerie stood off to the side watching in amazement. I could tell she was shocked about the story. There'd been rumors around school about the Bling Ring, but no one had ever confirmed anything. Well, that was about to change. They thought the cheerleading story was bad? I was in rare form. Wait until I finished this.

"And we're back in three, two . . ." Manny pointed to me and I began talking.

"Welcome back to *Rumor Central*, where we get the dirt on the celebs you love. Someone dial up Miami PD and tell them to take note because *Rumor Central* is on the case. And we're not spreading rumors today. We've got some cold, hard evidence. Video, from the notorious Bling Ring. And what better way to tell you than to show you. Roll tape."

The whole studio grew silent as the video of the three giggling teens running all throughout Shaq's mansion filled the monitor. They'd blurred the faces—legal said something about them being underaged. Still, I envisioned Bali at home, having a serious meltdown. But I don't know what he'd be upset for. He was the one doing the filming and had never turned the camera around on himself so no one could ever tie him to anything.

I let the video play a few minutes. Blake was making lewd gestures toward the camera with several of Shaq's championship trophies. The two girls were jumping up and down on an expensive-looking leather sofa as they laughed and poured champagne on the carpet.

"Take a good look," I continued as they made their way into Shaq's kitchen and began tossing food out, guzzling beer and spraying mustard everywhere. "*Rumor Central* obtained the exclusive video—and while we haven't been able to specifically identify the teens, rumor has it that they all hail from Miami's elite. One, reportedly, is hip-hop royalty, another is heir to a real estate dynasty, and the other is a prominent businessman's child. That's right, these bad teens could easily buy the stuff they're stealing. But we've learned they're not in it for the money, they're in it for the thrill. And don't

look for these crafty crooks to get caught anytime soon because I heard it through the grapevine that the Bling Ring is
security savvy and they know their way around some security
systems. So good luck to the Miami PD in tracking down
these home invaders. Holla at your girl if you need some
help." I laughed. I only added that because the legal department had told me I wouldn't have to talk to police because
they had everything covered. "Of course, *Rumor Central* will
stay on the case and keep you posted when more gossip hits
the fan."

I tossed to a commercial break, came back, and finished
out the show. After signing off, I prepared for the praise I
knew was headed my way.

Dexter did not disappoint, meeting me in my dressing
room with a big, cheesy grin on his face.

"Girl, you are the bomb-dot-com," he said.

I rolled my eyes at his attempt at being hip, but he didn't
seem fazed. "I can't wait to see what you come up with next.
Good job, Maya."

I half-smiled as he left the room. *What I came up with next?*
The problem was I didn't know how I could keep this rumor
mill going. But I knew no matter what, I needed to figure
out a way.

Chapter 20

I sat across the table from Tamara, toying with my pen, my mind a million miles away. I was thinking about Bryce and Sheridan. The homecoming dance was coming up and I couldn't believe he was going to take her. We'd talked about what we were going to wear and everything. Now, it looked like I wouldn't even get to go because no way would I go and have to look at their mugs all night.

"Maya, are you with me?"

"Huh?" I said, snapping out of my daze.

"I was just saying, it seems like you're not all here. And obviously, I was right." Tamara set her pen down and leaned back in her chair. "So, what has you so preoccupied?"

I hesitated. "Nothing. Really."

"Maya, I know I'm a few years older than you." She flashed a sly smile, probably because she knew she was a whole lot older than me. "But, I'd like to think that we can be friends."

I let out a long sigh. It was hard maintaining my divatude 24-7. Sometimes, I just wanted to let my hair down and tell someone what was really going on. There was something about Tamara that made me feel like I could do that, so I said,

"I don't know. Just kinda bummed about the way everyone at school is trippin' like I'm the one who is out of order for doing these stories."

"That's understandable." She patted my hand reassuringly. "Did you know Oprah Winfrey, one of the most powerful women in the world, even had her time when she struggled with people not liking her?"

"Someone doesn't like Oprah?" I asked.

Tamara nodded. "Yep. And at the end of the day, she just had to do her and forget all the haters."

"I mean, I'm used to the haters," I replied. "It's just that, well, this is on a different level."

"Maya, honey. It's only just beginning. Your star is rising, so it's only going to get worse." The look on my face must've made her feel bad because she began sifting through some papers. "But, I've got something that's sure to turn around those attitudes at your school."

I raised an eyebrow as I waited for her to find what she was looking for.

"Here it is."

"Here what is?" I asked.

She pushed a piece of paper toward me. It had a record company logo at the top and the title said DRAKE INTERVIEW/CONCERT.

"Wow, we have an interview with Drake?" Drake was not only one of the hottest rappers out, he had to be one of the cutest. Almost every girl at my school was crushing on him.

"No, honey. *You* have an interview with Drake," Tamara said.

Now that definitely lifted my spirits.

"But that's not the best part."

I couldn't believe it could get any better than me doing a one-on-one with Drake.

"His record company wants to do a private concert for a local high school," Tamara said.

"Why?"

"The whole connecting with fans, remembering the people who made him what he is, yada, yada," she replied.

"Okay, and?" I was super excited about the Drake interview, but I didn't see where Tamara was going with this.

"And what better high school than the one the host of *Rumor Central* attends?" she continued.

I studied her for a minute, then said, "Why would I want to give those busters at my school anything?"

"Because you'll have the last laugh," she said like it was a no-brainer. "Who can hate on Maya when she's bringing Drake to school?"

"I mean, I'm venting to you, but I don't care if they don't like me or not," I said.

She smiled like she really didn't believe me. "That's not the point. The point is you'll show these people that you always come out on top. You'll show Sheridan and Shay and everybody else that at the end of the day, you're the one with the juice."

"Oooo-kay," I said, finally getting where she was coming from. "So, is this a done deal?"

She took the paper back and put it in a folder on her desk. "Well, I'll have my secretary contact your principal to run this by him."

"Oh," I groaned. "Then we can forget it, because Mr. Carvin hates me."

"Oh, did I mention that the reason they want to do a high school is because they are bestowing a grant in Drake's name. The record company is donating the money."

"The money doesn't faze Mr. Carvin," I replied. "The kids at my school are rich."

"Yeah, the money might not faze him, but the publicity does," Tamara said. She didn't seem the least bit worried. "So, we'll go all out. We'll do a big rally, the concert. You'll introduce Drake, the whole nine."

A school concert? I was starting to feel what she was saying, but I still didn't see how this would go over with Mr. Carvin. "I just don't know," I said.

"You'll see. This is going to be off the chain!"

I laughed. Tamara and her whole crew needed some slang lessons 101.

"Okay, if you say so."

"I say so." She held up her palm to give me a high-five. I did, smiling at how she'd made me feel a hundred times better. "Now, let's get back to work," Tamara said.

Chapter 21

I had a headache and was dead tired, but I sucked it up and did my diva strut across the parking lot. I tried to do a cute yawn as I made my way down the hall to my third period (yeah, I knew I was super late, but I simply couldn't make it to school for first and second periods).

This juggling work and school was taking its toll, especially when you throw in all that it took for me to stay this fab—French manicures, keratin treatments, skin exfoliating, facials—all of that was time consuming. I made a mental note to see if I could "test out" of the rest of the semester. Yeah, I know no one had ever done that before, but I'd seen something about that on TV and if you asked me, I thought it was past time my school implemented something like that.

I had just turned the corner when I heard Valerie call my name.

"Maya!" she said, running toward me. "Where have you been? I've been trying to get in touch with you. Why aren't you answering your phone?"

I glanced at my phone, which was vibrating in my purse. I stopped and pulled out my iPhone. I grimaced when I saw the text from Tamara.

Where are u? Been waiting 20 minutes!!

Dangit! I'd forgotten all about our meeting this morning. I knew Tamara was going to be mad at me. She was actually meeting me at school this morning to do the presentation to the principal for us to host the Drake concert at Miami High.

"I gotta go," I said, making an immediate U-turn to head to the main building, where I was supposed to meet Tamara.

"Wait," she called out. The tone of her voice made me stop in my tracks.

"What's up, Valerie? I'm late. I was supposed to meet Tamara twenty minutes ago."

She looked at me strangely. "So, you're okay?"

"Yeah, why wouldn't I be?" I massaged my temple. Dang, I had a serious headache. I'd gone to a party last night for the premiere of this new reality show. I wish Kennedi or even Lauren had been able to roll with me, but both of them had something to do. So, I just told myself I was there to network and meet people and once Tamara showed up and started introducing me to everyone, I was cool.

"Wow. You don't seem fazed," Valerie continued. "I just thought . . ." She let her sentence trail off.

"If you're talking about Bali being upset about my story, I knew that was coming and don't care." Bali's maniac behind had texted me all day yesterday after he'd seen the Bling Ring story. He'd threatened me in all kinds of ways. I'd deleted the first two, but then saved the others so I would have them if I needed them. "I told you. I'm not trippin' off them."

"No, that's not what I'm talking about." I finally noticed that she looked all frazzled.

"Valerie, what is wrong with you?" I asked. "I need to go. Tamara is going to go nuts about me making her wait."

"Obviously, you haven't seen this," Valerie said, handing me her phone.

"Seen what?" I asked, taking the phone. I was about to

tell her how all this shock-and-secrecy crap was working my nerves when I looked at her screen. My mouth fell open. There on her phone was a picture of me with my goodies all out for the world to see. I almost dropped the phone in horror. I was wearing a hot pink lace pair of panties and nothing more. At least my hands were covering my breasts, but I was leaned into the camera, my lips puckered up. That picture had been sent to Bryce and had been for Bryce's eyes only.

"How did you get this?" I exclaimed.

"Everybody got them."

I looked up at her like she was speaking a foreign language. "What do you mean, *everybody* got them?"

"Someone texted them."

"What does that mean? Who?" She might as well have been speaking Swahili because I had no clue what she was talking about.

"Just what I said," Valerie replied. "I was with my friend, Jennifer and we got it at the same time. I saw you come on campus and left my class to come show you."

I glanced back down at the picture like it was going to disappear or something. "Who did the text come from?"

"I don't know. It came from an anonymous number. I tried to call it back, but the number was blocked. Everybody got it at the same time."

"Who is *everybody*?" I shouted.

"Everybody, everybody. The whole school, it seems."

I had to take slow breaths to keep from passing out.

"I only sent this to Bryce," I found myself muttering.

"Do you think Bryce did this?" she asked. "I know the two of you were dating and I saw him out by the gym on my way here. He was standing around laughing it up with his friends, so maybe . . ."

I didn't give her time to finish as I took off. I didn't need to think about who'd done this. Bryce's dog-behind. I knew we'd broken up, but I couldn't believe he was going to go out like that.

I spun around and headed toward the gym. Tamara would just have to wait a little while longer.

"Hey, wait up, Maya. Where are you going?" Valerie called out behind me.

I had never walked so fast in my stilettos, but I didn't plan on stopping until my four-inch heel was planted squarely in Bryce's neck. I spotted him immediately standing by the track, his friends gathered around him. There was no doubt what they were talking about the way they were all giggling and then backed up when they saw me approaching.

"Maya!" Bryce said, shocked as I barreled toward him.

"You low-down, dirty dog." Before I knew it, I had my shoe off and I was hitting him all upside the head. His boys were laughing like crazy. "I can't believe you did that!" I screamed.

"Stop it!" he said, trying to duck my blows. "I didn't do anything."

I kept hitting his lying behind.

"Maya!"

This time my name was being yelled from some other place.

"Maya!"

I stopped long enough to look up to see Tamara standing over me. The assistant principal, Mrs. Young, came rushing up right behind her.

I was so angry, I was on the verge of tears, but I refused to let Bryce see me cry. He was definitely going to see my anger though.

"I didn't do it," he said, all out of breath. He used the reprieve to jump out of my way. That didn't stop me. I lunged at him.

Mrs. Young jumped in the middle of us, stopping me from connecting my shoe with his head again.

"Have you two lost your minds?" Mrs. Young screamed.

"Oh, he's about to lose something, all right," I said, swinging at him. "His left eye."

This time it was Tamara who pulled me away. "Maya what in the world is going on?"

I didn't reply. I didn't know how she was going to take the photos. Besides, I was too upset to talk anyway.

"Seriously, Maya," Bryce pleaded. "I don't know how—"

"Shut up, you liar!" I screamed before Tamara grabbed me to keep me from going at him again.

Mrs. Young was on her walkie-talkie radioing for help. I guess she didn't want to get in the middle of a fight because she didn't jump back in the middle of us.

"Maya, you are on the verge of superstardom," Tamara whispered in my ear. "What in the world are you doing? Have you lost your mind? What about the Maya brand we're building? Are you trying to throw that away?"

Those words stopped me in my tracks. I looked at the crowd that was gathered around, laughing hysterically—of course a few of them were recording the whole thing on their camera phones. I'd probably be on YouTube before I got off campus.

Valerie eased up beside Tamara. "This is what has her so upset," she said, sticking out the phone to show her the photo. *Who asked Valerie to get involved?*

Tamara glanced down, but then looked back up at me. "Okay, and?"

I was a little stunned by her reaction. I'd expected her to light into me.

"They're naked photos of me," I cried. "They're probably all over Twitter and Instagram now. He sent them out to everyone." I jabbed my finger in Bryce's direction.

"I didn't do it," Bryce protested. "I swear. And I never showed them to anyone."

"Whatever, Bryce," I shouted. "You were the only person I sent those to."

By this point, two gym teachers came racing over. They immediately went to Bryce, who started trying to explain what was going on.

Mrs. Young walked over to me, anger all over her face.

"Young lady, you have caused so much trouble on this campus recently. I don't understand what—"

"Please," Tamara said, stopping her. "Just let me talk to her a moment."

Mrs. Young hesitated, but then must've decided she'd much rather Tamara deal with me, because she said, "Fine," before stepping aside.

Tamara grabbed my arm and pulled me off to the side. She lowered her voice and whispered, "Maya, do not do this. You are too fab to be acting like some kind of hood rat."

I raised my eyebrows. Maya Morgan and hood rat didn't even belong in the same sentence. But then, I looked down at my shoe in my hand and thought she had a point. I quickly eased my stiletto back on my foot. I tossed my hair over my shoulders and inhaled deeply to calm myself down.

"Let me tell you something," Tamara said. "First of all, they're not naked pictures. You have your panties on."

I narrowed my eyes at her. *Really?* Was that supposed to make me feel better? She ignored me and kept talking. "Have you ever heard the phrase 'no publicity is bad publicity'? So what, he sent the picture out. The bottom line, think Kim Kardashian, Paris Hilton. What are they all famous for? How bad did some video and pictures hurt them?" She didn't give me time to answer. "It didn't hurt them. If anything, it's the reason that you know their names."

"So, I'm supposed to be okay with this?"

"Of course, if we had our way we wouldn't put this out there, but it's out there now. Don't ever do this again. But when life hands you lemons, you make lemonade. I'll have our PR team all over this. We can even spin this and have you become a spokesperson for the dangers of social media." She seemed to get excited. "This isn't bad at all!" She held up Valerie's phone, which was still clutched in her hand and pointed it at me. "Look at that body. How many of these busted-looking chicks around your high school would kill for a body like that?"

I looked at the picture and I couldn't help but smile. I did look good. The Pilates had really paid off.

"This could be an album cover," Tamara continued. "You don't sing, but you're still a star. And this kind of stuff doesn't hurt stars. Shake that mess off. We're here to handle business. Don't let these peons at this school get to you."

I wanted to throw my arms around her neck. She was so right.

"Maya," Bryce said, approaching me. "I didn't—"

I held my hand up to stop him, but this time, I didn't yell. "Don't," I said. "Save it." I straightened my shirt and composed myself. "I should be used to people trying to ride my coattails to get a little fame," I snapped.

"I know you don't believe me, but I didn't send this out," he said.

"You're right, I don't believe you." I took a step closer. He flinched, like he was preparing for me to hit him again, but my hands went to my hips as I poked my chest out. "Take a good look, because this is the closest you will ever get to me again. Honestly, I understand. If Sheridan and her itty-bitty committee is all you have to work with, I'd be pulling up old pictures and salivating over them, too."

I glanced over at Tamara, who smiled her approval.

I knew Sheridan would hear about that flat-chested comment, but I didn't care.

"Now, if you'll excuse me," I said. "I have real business to
go handle."

"You dropped something," I heard Valerie say to Bryce as
she passed him.

"What, nerd?" he snapped. He was obviously upset about
the whole scenario.

"Your face. It's on the floor." Valerie giggled as she followed me and Tamara into the building.

Chapter 22

I'd finally pulled myself together and was now back to my fabulous self as we stood in front of the principal's office. I still didn't know how Tamara planned on working her magic and convincing Mr. Carvin to let us do anything. He'd made it clear that he despised *Rumor Central*.

"Keep the faith, honey," Tamara said confidently as Mr. Carvin's secretary gave us the go-ahead to go on back to his office. "This is what I do."

The minute we set foot in his spacious office, Tamara immediately turned on the charm. "Good afternoon, Mr. Carvin," she said, extending her hand. "Tamara Collins, WSVV-TV."

Mr. Carvin stood and shook her hand. He was wearing his usual bowtie and khaki slacks. "Ms. Collins, my pleasure." He eyeballed me. "Miss Morgan, were you just involved in some altercation?"

I looked at him innocently, but Tamara interjected. "It was all a big misunderstanding. Everything's fine."

"Yep, everything's fine," I replied with a fake smile. I'm sure he'd get all the details later, and he definitely wouldn't be happy. That's why Tamara needed to make her spiel, then we needed to keep it moving. Honestly, I didn't see why we were

wasting our time. Mr. Carvin belonged to the Maya Morgan
Hater Club.

Tamara took a seat in front of his desk and I sat next to
her. "Mr. Carvin, I am here on behalf of the station. As you
know, Maya is representing you well as host of our highly
popular show, *Rumor Central.*"

He squeezed his lips together, not bothering to look my
way as he said, "I would've preferred that you found another
capacity that Maya could represent us in."

Tamara didn't break her smile. "Understood, but know
that Maya is doing an awesome job"

He lost his smile, like he was tired of playing nice. "Ms.
Collins, what is it I can do for you? You said you only needed
about ten minutes." He looked at his watch. "And that's about
all the time that I have."

She crossed her long, curvy legs. I was surprised that Mr.
Carvin didn't seem to notice.

"Well, let me get straight to business. Since Maya is an in-
tegral part of our show, we'd like to include Miami High in
some of our promotional activities."

Mr. Carvin laughed, almost like he was insulted. "With all
due respect, Ms. Collins, Miami High is a prestigious school.
And neither our parents, nor our staff would take kindly to
being associated with a show such as *Rumor Central.*"

"Have you seen the show?" Tamara asked.

"I can't say that I have, but believe me, I've heard a lot
about it. And I've done my homework."

"Well, if you did your homework, you'd see *Rumor Central* has the highest ratings of any debut TV show in Miami.
That means that people are watching. And what better way
to garner publicity for your school than partnering with us?"

This woman was my she-ro. She wasn't about to be intimidated.

Mr. Carvin laughed again as he leaned forward onto his
desk. "I guess you're not hearing me, Ms. Collins, so let me

repeat myself. Miami High speaks for itself. We don't need the publicity."

"Miami High might not. But Mr. Russell Carvin could." She stood up and walked slowly around his desk, running her finger slowly over the desk, then walking over to his large bay window. "I understand you're nearing retirement," she said with her back to him.

The smile immediately disappeared from his face.

Tamara turned around, leaned against the window, and smiled. "I do my homework, too. And all I'm saying is what better way to go out than with a media blitz." It was obvious Tamara was getting through to Mr. Carvin because his face had turned red as he shifted uncomfortably in his seat.

"By allowing our partnership you can boost your enrollment," Tamara continued, walking back to the front of the desk, "bring attention to your school, raise money, and get round-the-clock media coverage."

Mr. Carvin was quiet for a minute, then finally said, "And just how would you do all that?"

Dang, Tamara was good. And she must've known it, too because she wasted no time, jumping right into her presentation. "We'd like to bring in a popular artist for a concert and list the school as a sponsor."

"Who are you trying to bring?" Mr. Carvin asked.

"Drake," Tamara replied.

Mr. Carvin looked horrified. "Isn't that a gangsta rapper?"

"He is a platinum-selling rapper," Tamara said. "But I assure you, he doesn't do gangsta rap."

I felt the need to add my two cents. "Mr. Carvin, Drake is one of the hottest rappers in the country right now."

"And anything he does here would be clean," Tamara added.

Mr. Carvin shook his head. "I'm not sure about this."

"Trust me," she said confidently. "Tell you what. I'll send over a package that gives you some info about the artist, as well as a detailed strategic plan on how this will benefit you. After you see that, you can make a final decision."

That seemed to alleviate some pressure, because his shoulders relaxed.

"Okay, I can do that," he said.

Tamara picked up her purse, which she'd set on the floor near her seat. "I'll have those sent over first thing in the morning. And I'm sure you'll be satisfied."

He finally smiled at her. "You sure are the confident one."

Tamara returned his smile. "What other way is there to be?"

They shook hands and I stood awkwardly to see if Mr. Carvin was going to say anything to me. Of course, he frowned when he looked my way. "Miss Morgan, have a good day. And please, try to stay out of trouble."

"Thanks," I mumbled as I followed Tamara out of the office.

"Dang, you handled him," I told her once we were heading out to the parking lot.

She shrugged like it was nothing. "Oh, he's small potatoes."

"Well, you served him up, fried and smothered in cheese," I laughed. I stopped suddenly when I saw Bryce heading toward me. The look on my face must've made him think twice because he paused, then turned around and walked in the other direction.

"Are you sure you're going to be okay?" she asked as she watched me watch him walk away.

I nodded, exhausted from all that had jumped off. The look on my face must've concerned her because she said, "I told you, don't sweat those pictures. They really aren't that bad."

I felt myself getting angry again, but quickly pushed it aside. "It's cool."

"Unh-unh," Tamara said. "That sounds like an 'it's cool,

I'm gonna get him back.' " She squeezed my arm. "Remember something my mom used to always tell me: 'Don't worry about getting back at those who wronged you. Success is the sweetest revenge.' "

I heard what she was saying, and I definitely planned to succeed, but I also planned to exact a little revenge of my own. I just didn't know how right now, but it was only a matter of time before Bryce learned the hard way what happened when people messed with me.

Chapter 23

Thoughts of revenge were fresh on my mind as I filed into my last class of the day. I was so ready to get home. I'd thought about skipping seventh period altogether, but I didn't need Mrs. Watson calling my parents and giving them something else to trip about.

"Settle down! Settle down!" Mrs. Watson said, ushering everyone into the room. Once we were all settled in our desks, she continued talking. "Now you know we're nearly at the end of the first semester. Some of you are fine and doing well with your grades. Others"—Mrs. Watson made a strange face—"well, you're not so fine. And remember, graduation may be months off, but every grade counts."

I groaned because she had to be talking about me. Her class was needed for graduation, and every chance she got, she reminded us of that.

She walked around her desk with a stack of papers in her hands. The papers were our fifteen-page research term papers that counted for more than half of our grades. As she moved to the left corner of the room, I remembered the stress I'd felt over that report.

It may not have been my very best work, but I'd managed to get it in, and I thought it had turned out pretty good considering I'd waited until the last minute and been up until nearly three in the morning trying to get it done.

"So, if you have any questions about your grade, comments, or anything else, email me for an appointment," she said.

The chatter had started back up and nearly drowned out her voice.

"Quiet down, and when you get your paper back, you may leave," she said, raising her voice.

That announcement was met with cheers. I sat quietly because I needed her to hurry up. There were tons of things for me to do with the show and even though I understood the importance of this class and the others, I was already getting on-the-job, hands-on experience in my field, so it was hard to stay focused on this mess.

Mrs. Watson began to flip through the stack. She looked down the row as if she was counting the students seated in front of her. She fingered the edges of the papers; then she separated the ones she needed and passed them out one by one.

"Score!" a student yelled enthusiastically.

"Awesome! Dude, what'd you get?" another student asked someone else.

I watched all of this while I prayed. I knew I needed at least a B, but I could manage with a C. A D would cause major problems.

Slowly the teacher moved from the first row, to the second. After she passed papers back to students in that row, she moved on to the third row. I sat in the last row near the end.

When she walked over and stood at the front of my row, I suddenly wished she was just starting at row one. All of my confidence in the work I had done instantly disappeared.

I watched in absolute horror as the student in front of me reached the papers back. With a trembling hand I grabbed them before they fell to the floor.

My throat went dry and I felt my eyes begin to burn. My vision was blurred, and it wasn't until I heard the voice behind me that I realized I had stopped and stared for too long.

"Heeello!" the girl behind me snapped.

"Oh, my bad." I quickly passed the last three term papers over my shoulder. I didn't even bother looking back because the girl behind me was one of the smartest kids in my school, so I knew that she'd aced the report. I took a deep breath, then looked at my paper.

Never in all of my years in school had I ever seen an F on a paper. The room began to spin, and I wanted to puke. Didn't an F mean you'd done absolutely nothing at all? How could I have gotten an F?

People around me began shuffling out of their chairs and it seemed like everyone else was happy with their grades. I didn't have any friends in class anymore that I could ask or confide in, so I had to assume that I was the only one who had flunked.

The word didn't even sound right swimming around in my head.

Maya Morgan flunked a class.

Maya Morgan flunked a grade.

Maya Morgan flunked.

"Eh-hem!"

Mrs. Watson's voice shattered my daze and that was when I realized we were alone in the room. I glanced around and wondered how everyone had left the room and I had never even noticed.

"Are you shocked by your grade or something?" Mrs. Watson asked.

I glanced back down at the paper and tried to find my

voice. I couldn't understand why we even had to do this crap. Shakespeare, really? That man died like a trillion years ago and I didn't need to know anything about Shakespeare to be an entertainment mogul.

Okay, so the paper sucked. I still didn't deserve an F because I had turned the assignment in on time. That, alone, should've given me at least a D. Yeah, I know I had waited until the last minute and had to stay up nearly all night, and I hadn't gotten a chance to review the work before I'd turned it in, but I still didn't deserve a freakin' F. Mrs. Watson wasn't fooling anyone. She'd done this because she hated me. Even the teachers were hating on me.

"What? You, Miss Chatter Box, are suddenly at a loss for words?" Mrs. Watson said. It was like she was enjoying my pain.

"Ummm, I kinda am," I muttered.

"Oh, no, don't whisper now," Mrs. Watson said.

Her voice was peppered with sarcasm and I didn't have the energy to fight with her or anyone else. I didn't have time to be worried about a stupid grade. There was a red-carpet event in a few days and that's where all my focus was. That, and trying to figure out how the heck I was going to make Bryce pay.

"When you're doing your TV show, you're a very confident and outspoken voice. Where's that voice today?" Mrs. Watson asked with her eyebrows raised.

She got up from her desk and walked to the row next to mine. She sat two chairs up from me in that row.

"Maya, you're way smarter than this. I know this show is very important to you, but I can't allow you to skate through my class when your peers are working twice, sometimes three times as hard as you," she said.

"But an F, Mrs. Watson?" Maybe I could appeal to her soft side (although I didn't even know if she had one).

She turned up her lips. "Well, to be honest, if there was something less than an F that I could have given you, I would have."

"What?" I exclaimed.

"Yes, if I could've given you a complete zero, or something less, I would have," she said.

Ouch!

I instantly wished I had shuffled out of the class right along with everyone else. I didn't need to sit and be ripped by my teacher. I needed to try and think about what dress I'd wear, or whether I'd meet my hair stylist and makeup artist at my house or at the event.

"I tried my hardest on this paper," I said, channeling my inner actress. "I gave this paper everything I had. That's why I'm so stunned at my grade." My chest heaved and I made myself cry (which wasn't all that hard because the thought of not graduating was enough to make me burst out into tears). But my theatrics, which normally worked on my parents, weren't moving Mrs. Watson.

"You're not being truthful, Maya," she said, pointedly.

"Well, I thought I had done what I was supposed to. I mean, if you've done one paper . . ."

She stopped me before I could continue. "Maya, you didn't even do a spell check. Your own name was misspelled. There were sloppy errors any Microsoft program would've caught." Mrs. Watson shook her head. "No, I'm sorry. You can't make me believe that you tried one bit. I felt like this paper was a complete afterthought for you, like the deadline snuck up on you and you rushed and slapped something together. This was completely unacceptable," she said.

I decided I couldn't win. I'd let her finish making her point and get in the jabs she wanted, then I'd be free to go. Mrs. Watson and everyone else would see a different side of me once I became super famous. Graduation wasn't that far off anyway so I only needed to indulge her for a few more months and I'd be on my way to bigger and better things.

I glanced back down at the big fat red F that was circled on my paper and swallowed back tears.

"Maya, your diploma is on the line here," she said. "I know you have your job and all, but how would it look if you're on TV, repeating the twelfth grade this time next year?"

My eyes widened. Would she seriously keep me from graduating?

"W-what can I do?" I so hated groveling, but since it was no one in the room but us, I would make an exception. "I can't fail this class." A part of me wanted to bribe her. Shoot, I heard teachers make like five dollars an hour. Surely, she could use some extra money. But Mrs. Watson's mean behind seemed like a bribe wouldn't do anything but make her madder, so I kept my mouth closed and waited on her to answer.

She hesitated, thinking. For a minute, I didn't think she was going to give me a chance, but finally, she said, "I'm not sure, but maybe if you start coming in after school immediately you can make up enough to fix your grade and make it across the stage."

I was just about to ask her whether we could start after the red-carpet event, but she quickly added, "The choice is yours."

Mrs. Watson got up and walked back to her desk, where she grabbed her purse and left the room. And based on the look on her face, I knew I really didn't have a choice at all.

Chapter 24

My life should really not be this difficult. I mean, I'm sure Beyoncé doesn't have this kind of drama from her parents.

So, I couldn't understand why I was standing here getting grilled by my mom. Dang, my dad had gotten all on my case just a few days ago. Now here I was again. I wish my parents could've gotten together, made some notes, and done all of this at one time. But since my mom was standing there with her lips all scrunched up and her arms folded across her chest, this was not the time to let her know I wasn't in the mood for a lecture.

"Maya, what in the world is this?" my mom said, pointing to the computer screen. I leaned in and peered over her shoulder.

"I . . . I—I don't know," I stammered once I saw what had her so upset. I was cold-busted and couldn't think up a lie fast enough.

She turned around and glared at me. "You know what it is. Your history teacher said you didn't turn in your last two homework assignments, one of which was a major part of your grade. First, you get suspended from school, now this? What in the world is going on?"

I was tired. I'd had enough grief from Mrs. Watson. Juggling the show, school, and staying fabulous was taking its toll, and I just didn't have the energy to come up with another story. I decided to come clean. "Mom, I just need to do a little catching up at school. It's no need to trip. I've been busy. The show has me swamped."

My mother narrowed her eyes at me and looked sternly my way.

"Now, when you said you were taking this job on, you said you could balance it with your schoolwork."

"And I can," I protested.

"Not according to this you can't!" She tapped the screen. "Not when you're not turning in your homework."

And failing English, I thought. "Awww, Mom." I so wanted to cut this conversation short and go crawl straight into bed. I'd been shooting promos all day, then I'd had to make a public appearance at a celebrity event and I was just exhausted.

"Don't 'awww, Mom' me. I have enough to deal with without having to worry about whether you're doing your schoolwork or not," she exclaimed. Of course she would make this about her. My mom acted like the sun rose and set around her. And exactly what did she have to deal with? Tennis? The spa? Brunch with friends? Junior League?

She must've finally noticed my appearance because she added, "And what in the world is all that on your face?"

"It's called makeup," I groaned.

She snatched a Kleenex out of the box on the counter and dabbed at my lips. "Wipe some of that makeup off, and who do you think you're getting smart with?"

I ducked my head out of her way. "I'm not getting smart. You asked me a question. We have to wear this for TV." I wished there was a button I could push to make myself disappear. Better yet, make my mom disappear.

My mom tossed the tissue in the trash, then rolled her

eyes as she shut down her laptop. "I can see now that this job is going to be a problem."

"No, it's not, Mom." The last thing I wanted was getting her riled up so I just agreed. "Okay, okay. I promise I'm going to buckle down at school." The station wanted to send me to the MTV Awards next month in Los Angeles, so the last thing I wanted was my mom tripping and telling me I couldn't go because of some stupid grades.

"Get it together, Maya," she warned as I made my way out of the kitchen.

I blew a frustrated breath and started heading up the stairs to my room before she found something else to gripe about. My cell phone rang just as I plopped down on my bed. I almost didn't answer it because the phone number came up as blocked, but I knew every time Tamara called me from her office the number came up blocked. It was probably her checking on me, so I decided to answer.

"Hello," I said.

"Maya, don't hang up," Bryce quickly said.

I groaned at the sound of his voice. He'd been blowing up my phone, sending me text messages apologizing and swearing over and over that he hadn't had anything to do with sending out my picture.

"What do you want, Bryce?" I asked. I don't know why I didn't just hang up. I guess a part of me wanted to understand how he could do something like that with my pictures. I needed to know if he really hated me that much. Not that I cared, but if so, it meant that he'd never really cared for me in the first place. I had really been feeling Bryce when we were together. I guess you could say even though I'd played hard to get, he was my first love. So for him to go there really hurt.

"Why are you bothering me anyway?" I continued. "Does your girlfriend know you're calling me?"

"Sheridan is not my girlfriend," he protested. "We're just . . ."

"Are you going to the homecoming dance with her or

not?" I asked, cutting him off. I noticed a picture the two of us had taken last month in one of those cheesy mall photo booths. We were acting silly, something I rarely did. But Bryce brought out the fun side of me. I'd loved just letting my hair down with him.

I stood, walked over to the picture, snatched if off the mirror, then dropped it in the trash.

"Well, yes, but it's because—"

"Then, whatever, Bryce. Save it." I fell back across my bed.

He sounded panicked. "No, I'm trying to tell you, yeah, Sheridan and I are kickin' it, and she's cool and all, but I don't love her like I love you."

Those words made me sit straight up in my bed. In our entire three months together, Bryce had never uttered those words to me.

"*Love me?* Since when?"

"Since I lost you," he said softly.

I wanted to tell him that he hadn't *lost* me, he'd *dumped* me but since those words would never, ever leave my mouth, I remained quiet.

"I'm just saying, I miss you, boo."

I felt myself getting sucked in by his words, so I quickly shook myself out of my trance. "Bryce, *miss* me with that foolishness because I'm not even buying it. You're the only person I sent that picture to so you had to have sent it to everybody."

"I know you don't believe me, but I would never do anything like that. I mean, I'm happy for your success. I wouldn't try to mess you up like that. If anything, I wish I could be a part of all your success."

You could have been, I wanted to say. Now, he had a better chance of getting with Beyoncé.

"All I'm saying is, I don't want you believing I would do something like that," he continued.

The strange part is that had been what didn't make sense about all of this. Sending that picture was just not Bryce's character. But still, if he hadn't done it, who had?

I decided to ask. "Then how did the picture get out if you didn't send it, Bryce?"

"I don't know. I've been racking my brain thinking about it," he replied. "It's on my phone, but you know I keep my phone with me at all times." He paused like he was recalling something. "Except . . ."

"Except what?"

"Except the other day when Sheridan was over my house and my mom called me outside to help her bring the groceries in," he slowly began. "I left my phone sitting on the coffee table." He sounded like he was thinking. "When I came back, I was a little shocked because the light on the phone was on. Sheridan told me it had rung, only I didn't see a missed call."

"So you just left it alone and took her word for it, huh?"

"Nah, my mom was trippin' and I was distracted. That had to have been what happened. Sheridan had to have seen the picture and sent it to herself when I was dealing with my mom."

"How convenient. Your girlfriend is the one who sent the picture out, not you," I said, my voice filled with sarcasm. "Yeah, right." But even as I was shooting his explanation down, my gut told me that Bryce was right on the money. Sending that picture to everyone was a Sheridan move if I had ever seen one. But still, I wasn't cutting Bryce any slack.

"Not that I believe you. But if I did, it doesn't matter anyway. You and Sheridan are both losers. So lose my number," I said, pressing the button to end the call.

Sheridan Matthews. She was the one behind this! "You conniving little wench," I mumbled. Bryce was a lot of things, but he was never dirty like that. But that was classic Sheridan.

I picked up the phone and punched in her number. I hadn't called her since I'd started working at *Rumor Central*, but I needed to give her a piece of my mind. Her phone rang twice before she picked up.

"Somebody must've stolen this phone because I know Maya Morgan isn't calling me," she answered with an attitude.

"No, only one person is in the phone-stealing business," I replied.

"What do you want?" she said like I was truly bothering her.

"You think you're slick," I began. I was so angry that I began pacing back and forth across the room. "I know it was you that sent out that picture of me on Bryce's phone."

"Whatever are you talking about?" she replied innocently. "Ooooh, you mean the *Playboy* bunny photo that you sent my boyfriend."

I bit down on my teeth to keep from going off. "He was *my* boyfriend when I sent it. And if he's your man now, why was he telling me how much he loves me five minutes ago?" I couldn't help but throw that in. "Maybe if you go stuff some tissue in your bra, you can take some pictures Bryce will want to carry around." I knew that would cut her since she was so self-conscious about her small breasts.

"Screw you, Maya! You're the only slut that takes dirty pictures," Sheridan screamed.

I debated going there with her, but I wasn't about to engage her. I just had a warning for her.

"Karma is no joke, Sheridan."

"Am I supposed to be scared?" she replied, calming down. "Yeah, you might have some dirt on me, but just remember, any dirt I did, you were right there with me as I was doing it."

She was so right about that. There were a few things about Sheridan I'd considered revealing, but I'd nixed each one of those ideas because that would've been incriminating myself as well.

"Don't even play me," Sheridan said. "You have nothing on me. And if I did send the little funky slutty picture, you need to be thankful that's all I did. With everything I know about you, I could make it where Bryce thinks you're the biggest whore in the whole state of Florida."

I was just about to reply when she added, "Don't call me again," before hanging the phone up in my face.

"Ugh!" I screamed, as I hurled my phone across the room. I was livid.

Sheridan Matthews didn't know who she was messing with. But I was definitely about to show her!

Chapter 25

Mrs. Watson was going to blow a gasket. I'd begged her to let me do the makeup work. Now, here I was about to miss yet another class. But I didn't have any choice. Tamara wanted me at the TV station to do another promo shoot. I knew I had to get it together because the last thing I needed was to mess up graduation behind this show. That's why I was speeding toward campus. It was just 11:45, so I could still go in to Mrs. Watson and plead my case.

I guided my BMW onto my school's street and immediately slowed at the sight of the cop cars lined up out front. We very seldom had any drama at Miami High. Not because there wasn't any drama, but because most of the kids' parents bailed them out of everything before any real drama jumped off. So it was a shock to see all the police officers.

"What's going on?" I asked after I had parked and made my way through the parking lot. The group of people I asked gave me the most hateful looks and didn't reply. "What?" I said to one of the girls.

Just then, I saw what the officers were doing as they carted out Amanda, Sabrina, and Blake. My mouth fell open.

Amanda saw me and immediately tried to break free from the police officers.

"I'm gonna kill you!" she screamed as they pulled her back. "I can't believe you did that, you snitch."

"Shut up, Amanda," Blake barked. "Don't say a word!" He shot me a look of pure evil, letting me know that he hated me just as much. Even though he'd stopped Amanda from attacking, the look on Blake's face said he'd give good money to let her have her way with me.

Okay, this was getting totally out of control. I was just trying to get ratings. I wasn't trying to get anyone arrested.

Before I could say anything, I spotted one of the few classmates that didn't have a beef with me. "Sandy, what's going on?"

"What does it look like? The Bling Ring got busted," she replied, shaking her head as she watched them push Blake into the car.

"Yeah, they got arrested, thanks to you," one of Sandy's friends said. "And they want to call me lame? At least I'm not a snitch," she said, before walking off.

"Don't pay her any attention," Sandy said. "But if I were you, I'd kinda lay low for a minute, because you're not exactly well liked right about now."

The way everyone was looking at me, I knew Sandy was telling the truth.

"I don't understand what everyone is mad at me for."

Sandy cut her eyes at me.

"You, too?"

"Naw, I understand. You're just doing your job. But brace yourself." She motioned up the sidewalk. "Here comes Mr. Carvin."

The principal stomped toward me and stopped right in front of me. "I need to see you in my office right now, young lady," he said firmly.

Part of me wanted to resist and tell him I wasn't going anywhere without my attorney, my parents, Tamara, or somebody. But the look in his eyes told me it wasn't up for discussion.

I followed him back into the office. He slammed the door and spun on me. "Do you have any idea the damage you are doing to this school's reputation?"

"By what? Reporting the news? I mean, you were all behind me when I was making you look good, and getting the school all kinds of publicity."

He took a deep breath like he was trying to weigh his words. "Holding a school concert is quite different from that gossip garbage you're spewing on television."

"No disrespect, but are you mad because they're doing it or because they were busted?" I asked. He was making me sick, trying to act all self-righteous.

He stood up straight like he was offended. "Of course I don't condone bad behavior, but when you shine a negative light on this school, I have to be concerned. And since you took on that show, that's all you've been doing."

"No, not once have I mentioned Miami High," I replied. "In fact, I made it a point not to mention the school."

"Well, the newspapers know. You didn't exactly make it hard for them to find out. I've been dealing with reporters all day."

"Well, that's beyond my control." I was having trouble understanding how I was the one making the school look bad. If anything, the cheerleaders, the Bling Ring, they were the ones making the school look bad.

Mr. Carvin took a deep breath like he was going to try another approach. "Look, Miss Morgan, I understand you think you have your dream job, but you're gaining notoriety at the expense of your friends."

"They're not my friends," I said.

He sighed like he was super frustrated. "Is this some personal vendetta? Are you mad because the school took away your newspaper job last year?"

"No. I think it's completely unfair how you let Ivory fire me from the newspaper staff."

I hadn't thought about that stupid job since I'd stopped working last year. I'd done entertainment reports and the editor, Ivory, had had the nerve to fire me because she said I didn't meet deadlines. Personally, I think she was just hating.

"You know I let you students run that newspaper. And even if you had stayed, you would've been fired because of the fight you had a few weeks ago," Mr. Carvin said. "You know the rules. You cannot be in any extracurricular activities if you're fighting."

"I wasn't fighting. I was defending myself," I protested. "But I guess I was just supposed to sit there and let Shay beat me up."

"You know the rules and just because you think you're some superstar doesn't make you exempt from the rules."

I stood. "Well, really, as you can see, I'm so over this little job at a school newspaper. I work for a real place. It's my job to report the news, as ugly as it may be."

"Miss Morgan, I'm warning you. You're making a very bad mistake." He lowered his voice and leaned in. "I am on the verge of retirement and I'm not about to let some wet-behind-the-ears spoiled brat ruin that!"

His tone actually caught me off guard. "Are you threatening me, Mr. Carvin?"

He stood up, straightened his jacket. "Of course not, Miss Morgan." His voice was back to sounding official. "That's ridiculous. I would never threaten a student," he said, much louder. "But I am warning you." He lowered his voice again. "You're making enemies left and right. And I don't think that's something you want to do. You have some powerful friends around here. Powerful friends from powerful families, so I don't think that making enemies is something that you want to do."

"Thank you for your concern." I headed out of the office. Luckily, government was one class where I had paid attention and I had the right to freedom of speech. So Mr. Carvin could trip all he wanted. I knew at the end of the day, there was nothing he could do to shut me up.

Chapter 26

When I walked out of the bathroom, my eyes were focused on my damp hands.

"Stupid air blower thingie," I muttered, wiping my hands on True Religion jeans. By the time I looked up, it was almost too late; I'd nearly stumbled over my own two feet. It wasn't because I had tripped on anything, but it was because of the two lovebirds that stood hugged up in front of me. My heart began to beat at a rapid rate. Just the sight of them made me sick to my stomach.

She was leaning with her back against the locker and he had his arms bent at the elbows, hovering over her head. He leaned in so close to her that there was no way he could've seen me coming.

I couldn't hear what she had whispered to him, but whatever she said made him drop his arms and turn to face me.

"What's up, Maya?" Sheridan had the nerve to say. She was grinning like I couldn't stand her guts.

Bryce just looked at me like he was some kind of idiot on steroids.

"Wow, Maya, so it's like that?" Sheridan said as she stepped closer to Bryce. "You're just going to ignore us?"

"Come on, Maya," Bryce added. "It's not . . ."

The look on my face caused his words to trail off. I stared at them. The sight of the two of them made my eyes burn. I couldn't stand looking at them, much less having them invade my space. This hallway, this campus, this city even wasn't anywhere near big enough for the three of us.

I pointed at my chest. "Were you talking to me, you shisty dog?" I asked Bryce. Sheridan would get no acknowledgment from me. "I mean, there was no way you could possibly be talking to me."

I walked back toward them, stopping a few feet away, and putting my hands on my hips.

"You don't get the privilege of ever uttering my name again, you sleazy, low-down dog," I spat to his face.

Bryce didn't flinch.

"Maya, really?" Sheridan huffed.

I spun on her. "I know you're not talking to me either," I said.

She flinched and that made me happy. The tramp didn't know if I was gonna spit or slap.

"You should really calm down, Maya," she said.

"I should slap the mess out of you, that's what I should really do, but then again, you're not even worth it," I said.

I turned and walked away.

"You two deserve each other," I said over my shoulder before I made it down the hall and away from the two maggots.

As I walked down the hall and toward my class, I was glad I'd stopped and said something. I realized I needed to get my frustrations off my chest.

I couldn't fathom what the heck Bryce saw in her. She was a total nobody, she lived in my shadow and obviously was so jealous of me that she'd found happiness and satisfaction with my sloppy seconds.

"Dang!" I rolled my eyes at my forgetfulness. I'd let Sheridan and Bryce rattle me and I didn't even get my book out of my locker.

See what the sight of those two did to me? I was all discombobulated. I'd avoided my locker, thinking I needed to keep it moving to blow off some steam. But the truth was I'd really needed to make that stop.

I pulled the classroom door open and strolled inside. It was my teacher's conference period before this class so I knew it'd be empty.

I placed a notebook on the desk I wanted and rushed back out to go to my locker.

My eyes focused in on something flapping in the wind. It was attached to my locker and I wondered what it could've been. When I approached and got close enough I realized it was that doggone picture of me in my lace undies. Somebody had actually printed it out and taped it to my locker.

I was firecracker hot!

"Ugh" I screamed, snatching the paper down.

A few heads turned.

Some people stared, but I didn't care.

I also didn't miss those who snickered. Who knew how long the picture had been taped to the outside of my locker. It was such a good thing that I hadn't seen this before. If I had come to my locker and found this, it would've been on in the middle of the hallway.

"I can't believe that nasty prick," I said as I snatched the picture down.

"What are you looking at?" I barked at one of my classmates who had walked up and was trying to get a closer look.

I balled the photocopy up. I wanted to kill Bryce and Sheridan! This was all their fault. If *he* understood boundaries, if *she* valued our friendship, none of this would've happened.

After I opened the locker and grabbed the book, it hit

me. I knew the perfect plan for revenge, at least for Sheridan. I'd been leaning against it, but all bets were off with this latest move.

I slammed the locker shut and rushed toward class with new inspiration. Finally, I'd get the last word, and the last laugh!

Chapter 27

When I sat at my desk and heard the two most dreaded words a teacher could utter, I couldn't imagine anything worse. A pop quiz that I wasn't prepared for seemed more than just unfair, it seemed downright wrong.

I looked around the crowded classroom. Why was I the only one who seemed unprepared? This had caught me completely off guard, but everyone else seemed just fine. Not a single other person seemed bothered.

"Okay, clear your desks, nothing but pencils," the teacher said.

I was so mad at him. A pop quiz should not have been part of the lesson plan, especially since I was so behind with my studying, and reading, and most things related to all my classes actually.

Everyone else eagerly cleared books, notepads, and papers from their desks.

I wanted to bolt from the classroom and never, ever come back. Where was a fire drill when I needed one? The teacher stood near the front of his desk and waited for everyone to appear ready.

I wondered if continuing to rummage through my book

bag would delay this pop quiz even more. The joke was on me because he apparently wasn't waiting on everyone, just most people. I still wasn't done looking through my bag when someone laid the pop quiz on my desk.

I kept a sheet, then passed the rest back behind me. When I glanced down at the paper, I wanted to cry. Nothing looked familiar! How far behind had I fallen?

The problems on the sheet of paper looked like a foreign language to me. But to my left, and to my right, heads were bowed and people were writing on their papers.

I reread the first question and my head began to hurt. When had we covered this?

I thought about falling onto the floor and faking a seizure, but the thought of my Gucci black silk dress touching the floor was enough to make me squash that idea real fast.

Suddenly a loud knock on the door pulled everyone's attention away from their papers.

Our teacher got up and walked to the door. When he pulled it open, two men in suits stood there. It wasn't until they flashed badges that I heard voices gasp in the classroom.

"Hi, I'm Detective Greene and this is my partner, Detective Peterson. We're here because we need to speak with one of your students," the man said.

Just then, the assistant principal, Mrs. Young, squeezed between them and walked into the room.

"Mr. Griggs, these officers need to talk with Maya Morgan," she said. Even though their voices were low, they sucked at whispering so everyone in the class heard them. When they turned and looked at me, I felt every eye in the room focus in on me, too.

"Maya, you need to go with these officers," Mr. Griggs said.

The whispers and chatter started instantly.

"OMG, what did she do?"

"Is she snitching, again?"

"This is too much!"

I slowly stood and made my way toward them. With each step I took, I felt like I was walking a plank, like I had done something wrong. I had no idea what they wanted, but just like everyone else in the room, I was sure it had something to do with either the Bling Ring or the cheer escort stories. I could only imagine that by the time the lunch bell rang, I'd be the center of tons of school gossip.

"Where's your quiz?" Mr. Griggs had the nerve to ask.

"I didn't get a chance to finish it," I stammered.

"Well, of course not, but turn in what you have so far," he said.

"Yeah, but I don't want . . ."

"Sir," one of the detectives said, acting irritated at our exchange.

Mr. Griggs stepped aside, glaring at me as I walked by and left the room with Mrs. Young and the detectives.

Tamara had already told me that if I was ever questioned about any of my stories, I needed to keep my mouth shut. But it had been a couple of weeks since the Bling Ring bust and nothing had happened. And as far as I knew, Evian and her crew hadn't even been questioned by police, so I'd thought I was in the clear with the cheer story. And I figured if they'd needed any information from me about the Bling Ring, it would've been right after they made their arrests.

"Is there an office we can use?" one of the detectives asked Mrs. Young.

"Oh, yes, come this way. We can talk in here," she said and guided us into a side door that led to a hall that connected the administrative offices.

I was grateful for that. The last thing I wanted was to be paraded in front of everyone who may have been in the main office. I was sure those busters in my class were already texting and tweeting that I'd left to talk to cops, but I didn't need everyone all up in my business any more than necessary.

After I was seated at the small conference table, the first detective immediately began talking.

"Miss Morgan, we won't hold you long. We just have some questions about the so-called Bling Ring. We need to know if you have ever heard your classmates talk about the Royal Oaks subdivision?"

"I don't know anything more than what I said in the story," I said.

They looked at each other.

"But around campus you never heard them talk about some of the places besides houses that belonged to celebrities?" the second officer threw in.

"I didn't know any of those students," I lied. "I mean, sure we all attend the same school, but this is a big campus. All I did was follow the tips that led to what was going on." Yeah, I'd shared their business with the station, but I wasn't about to give the cops any additional information. I had enough folks out for blood from me as it was.

"Miss Morgan, if you know anything about these crimes, you have an obligation to tell us," the first detective said.

I shrugged. "I wish I could tell you something, but I don't know anything."

Both of the detectives looked exasperated.

Mrs. Young nodded. I didn't know if that was encouragement or a signal that I had done a good job. If I had known what was coming next, I would've dragged this questioning out a lot longer.

"Well, that's all we have for now. You can go back to class," one of the detectives said.

My head whipped in the direction of Mrs. Young.

She got up from the chair and rubbed her hands together.

"Okay, Maya, thank you. I will send you back with a slip," she said.

Back to class? That was the last place I wanted to go. Why hadn't they questioned me more? Should I yell out something to make them stay? Should I tell them about Bali? Naw, I couldn't stand him anymore, but I wasn't trying to get him thrown in jail. It was too late to do anything anyway because they were already up and headed toward the door.

I sulked behind Mrs. Young and followed her into her office. She gave me the slip and I left and headed back to class.

As I walked down the hall, I wished I was anyplace but school. I thought about just ducking out and going home, but Mrs. Watson's makeup test was next period and if I missed it, there would be no more chances. When I reached my classroom, I stopped outside and took a deep breath.

I knocked on the door and was highly disappointed when my teacher pulled the door open.

"Oh, Maya, that was quick, I didn't expect to see you again until tomorrow," he said, waving me in, then handing me my quiz back.

"Don't take long to rat someone out," someone yelled from the back of the room.

"Snitch!" another person said.

"That's why you have butt-naked pictures on Instagram!" someone else called out.

Mr. Griggs tried to settle everyone down, but I just tuned them all out. There was no point in wasting time trying to figure out who had said what. I knew they were probably saying what everyone else felt but couldn't bring themselves to say to my face.

Whatever, I told myself as I turned my attention back to the pop quiz I was destined to flunk.

Chapter 28

I couldn't believe the words that had just left Mrs. Watson's mouth.

"It's a once-in-a-lifetime opportunity. You can miss one day of the after-school makeup classes to go," Mrs. Watson said.

I was so stunned I could barely move. I'd just known I would have to cry, plead, and beg to get her to let me miss her makeup class to attend the Miami Film Festival.

"I'm not a total jerk," Mrs. Watson said with a smile. I wanted to give her a giant hug.

And the good thing about it all was I knew how good I looked, too. For all the hating I experienced at school, it was times like these that made me realize it was all worth it.

I was working the red carpet and the rest of those scrubs were fighting with paparazzi to get a front-row peek at all the action that was going down, including the *Miami Divas*, who had gotten an "exclusive invitation" to attend the event. Only thing was, that invitation hadn't been real. I had sent each of them fake letters that the *Miami Divas* were getting an award; I was counting on their egos to get them to show up. Bali, Sheridan, Shay, and Evian had been told to wait by the red-carpet entrance and a producer would come get them. I wanted to laugh out loud when I saw them still standing there, waiting, thinking someone was actually going to come get them.

We had planned to tape a segment for the show while I was working the carpet, so not only would they be sick because I'd be prancing up and down the red carpet, but they'd also get to relive that sickness again and again when the show aired.

I focused in on the camera's lens when my photographer got in position.

He said, "Standby. On four, three, two . . ." Then he pointed at me.

"I'm Maya Morgan and I'm here on the red carpet," I began. "You don't have to worry about missing a thing from the Miami Film Festival because we've got you covered. I'll find out who's wearing whom, I'll tell you the dirt on who's showing up here with someone else's man, and you'd better believe it, I'm asking all the questions you want to know!"

I stood and held my smile so he could focus and get a few cutaway shots. From the corner of my eye, I caught a glimpse of Evian, Shay, Bali, and Sheridan's faces.

"Was that okay?" I asked the photographer, looking over at their grim faces.

"Yeah, it's cool," he said.

"Okay, can we get some MOSes?" I asked. Those were man-on-the-street comments, where we randomly selected people to ask questions.

"Oh, yeah, that'll work. Let's rock 'n' roll," he said.

I picked up the hem of my cascading ruffled dress and pranced over to the edge of the rope that cut off the little people from those of us who were important.

I saw the excitement in Evian's eyes as I got close. Like I would ever put them on camera.

They could try to front all they wanted, but they knew

the truth. The truth was they could hate and talk about me all they wanted, but deep down inside they all wanted to be me, or just like me.

I smiled as I made my way over to where they stood. There were a couple of other students standing right next to them.

"Is this good?" I asked the photographer.

He nodded.

"Who are you gonna talk to?" he asked.

When I turned to the crowd, I saw nothing but hungry, desperate eyes. While their lips never moved, everything about them said "choose me" or "pick me!" I put a perfectly manicured finger between my glossy lips like it might help me make the decision a little faster, then turned to face my nemeses.

One by one, I eyed each one and smirked when I settled on the little plain-Jane girl who had squeezed up to the front to be seen.

"Um, excuse me," I said. I was so glad she was standing right next to Evian. That meant Evian and the other two would be in the shot, but they'd be completely excluded from what was going on.

I stuck the microphone to her lips and the photographer adjusted his stance and camera.

"Okay, I'm rolling," he said.

I turned and said, "You are out here on the red carpet. Tell our viewers, who do you want to see most?"

"OHMYGOD! OHMYGOD! I can't believe you picked me. Am I on TV like, right now?" she asked.

I wanted to scream, but I knew by the evil eye I was getting from the eight sets to her left, that my plan had worked just fine.

We wrapped up the interview with the plain Jane; then we went on to record three more, all with people who stood next to, behind or near Evian, Sheridan, Shay, and Bali.

"Has the producer shown up to meet you guys yet?" I couldn't help but ask, before bursting out laughing as I walked away.

The looks on their faces said it all. They were outdone. They knew they had been played. Oh, they stood there with their arms crossed over their chests, and their faces mean-mugging the cameras, but what did I care? I looked fabulous and there was nothing any of them could do about it.

"That was great, Maya," the photographer said.

I beamed with pride.

"Here, let's go back and get our spot," he said as he grabbed the tripod from the bottom and carried it back to where we were.

Once I got back to my place on the red carpet, I couldn't help but steal glances over at my former friends. They had looks on their faces that said the grapes they were sucking on were oh so sour!

My composure was cool as a cucumber on the outside. But on the inside it was a completely different story. I was jigging all the way and loving every minute of it.

What could they say or do? While they were roped off and forced to fight for space with the hired help, yours truly was hosting the red-carpet affair. That meant they had to stand there and watch as each celebrity who passed schmoozed and chatted me up like I was Oprah (quiet as it's kept, give me around one year and I'll give Oprah a run for her money). But I guess they had all they could take, because I saw Sheridan spin off first. She pushed her way through the crowd, away from the Red Carpet. It only took a few seconds, but Bali, Evian and Shay quickly followed.

I fought back my laughter, then pushed them out of my thoughts. The feeling I had was so fantastic that I wanted us to stay on the red carpet the entire night. With bulbs flashing and paparazzi clicking pictures, I smiled and laughed like I was having the time of my life.

And for all intents and purposes, as far as at least four people could tell, that's exactly what I was doing. I was having the time of my life soaking up the spotlight that shone solely on me while they were forced to stand off to the side and occupy what little time they could squeeze in when and if a camera happened to pan in their direction.

"You ready to go inside?" the photographer asked.

"You know I am," I said and once again grinned hard for the cameras. "Sweetie, Maya Morgan stays ready," I added as I followed him inside.

Chapter 29

"All right, are you ready?" Dexter looked at me with a reassuring smile. He must've known that I was real nervous about this story. Watching my former friends outside the red carpet yesterday had been wonderful, but Sheridan's payback needed to go much deeper. And I had the shovel and was about to start digging!

I was so nervous that I hadn't told anyone about what was about to go down. Even Valerie didn't know about the blockbuster show that was in store for today. Not only was I going to bust Sheridan's self-righteous behind out, I was going to do it with a smile and supersized ratings.

"You need anything?" Valerie said, checking on me in my dressing room.

"Nah, I'm cool." I leaned into the wall-to-wall mirror and surveyed my reflection. I nodded my approval at Gina, the makeup artist. She started gathering up her supplies. I turned to face Valerie. She had been trying really hard to be not only a good assistant, but a good friend as well. And while I'd never consider us BFFs, I did actually like the girl.

Just not enough to stop me from doing this story.

"Just getting ready for the show." I hoped that Valerie didn't trip too hard after the show. She hated Sheridan as much as I did (although sometimes it seemed like she hated her more), so I couldn't see her being too mad.

"All right, break a leg," Valerie said.

I waited as the hair stylist put the finishing touches on my spiral curls. I made it to the set with just a few minutes to spare.

The director cued me. I took a deep breath and began my signature greeting.

"Hey, hey, hey, what's up? Welcome to *Rumor Central*, where we dish the dirt on the celebs you love, and boy, are we dishing some dirt today," I said, full of enthusiasm. I knew they loved my personality and I was totally bringing it. "I'm not one to gossip," I continued, "but rumor has it one of the biggest stars to ever come out of Miami took fame by any means necessary." I turned to the other camera in a dramatic fashion. "She is one of the country's hottest actresses. One of the world's highest paid singers. She has a clothing line, and *Forbes* named her one of the richest women in America. But have we got some dirt on Glenda Matthews." I paused for effect as a picture of a young, very pregnant Glenda Matthews popped up on the screen. Our research department had worked overtime to find the photo. I had to give them their props. They were no joke.

"Do you know who this woman is?" I said while the picture stayed up on the monitor. "Well, if you guessed Glenda Matthews, you guessed right. This was taken in 1996, when Glenda was pregnant with her first child. And this"—I waited for the next photo to pop up—"was taken in 1997. In it, Glenda was pregnant as well. But wait, you say, Glenda Matthews only has one daughter, seventeen-year-old Miami socialite Sheridan Matthews. So what happened to the kid from that 1997 picture? Well, that's what we wanted to know, too. *Rumor Central* has dug deep to find out that Glenda's second child, the one that she is pregnant with in this picture." I waited for the picture to pop up again. "The one whose father is a married rock star, the one who was apparently too much of an inconvenience. That child was born in 1997, just eleven months after the birth of her first child, and according to court records, Glenda gave the child up for adoption so she wouldn't lose her coveted role as Cleopatra in the 1998 blockbuster movie that put her on the map. *Rumor Central* hasn't been able to locate the child yet. But we did track down Ms. Matthews." The camera cut to a picture of Glenda Matthews running into her garage as the cameraman followed behind her, asking if the allegations were true.

As soon as the video stopped, I continued. "Last year, Glenda Matthews threw her daughter, Sheridan, a sweet sixteen party that was featured on MTV's *Super Sweet Sixteen* show as one of the top ten Sweet Sixteen bashes of all times. I was there so I can tell you it was all that and then some. But one can't help but wonder, did baby number two get a sweet sixteen party? Did the abandoned child of Glenda Matthews get to enjoy a life of luxury? Does she even know that her mother is one of the biggest stars in the country? We want to know just like you, and you'd better believe *Rumor Central* is all over this story. And if you want the scoop, make sure to keep it tuned right here."

We went to commercial break, came back, did some more local and national entertainment and celebrity stories, then finally wrapped up the show.

As soon as I signed off, Tamara and Dexter rushed onto the set.

"Oh my God, that was fabulous," Tamara said.

They weren't the only ones showering me with praise. I

knew I'd scored when the general manager walked in and said, "That's what I'm talking about. Absolutely phenomenal! I can't believe you're only seventeen. You have a long future in this business." He gave me a high-five, which caught me off guard. But while everyone else was celebrating, I noticed that Valerie stayed in the corner, giving me an evil teary eye.

"Hey, V. What's wrong?" I asked after everything had started dying down and people made their way back into their offices.

She shook her head in disbelief. Were those really tears in her eyes?

"I can't believe you did that," she said.

"Did what?"

"Don't play dumb, Maya!" she snapped, then quickly lowered her voice and looked around before leaning in and whispering, "I can't believe you ran with that story."

It was my turn to be shocked. *No, she isn't snapping at me.* "Why are you trippin'? You knew I was working on something big."

"Yeah, but I gave you that information." Her voice was actually trembling. "I shared it with you just for your ears, not to run it on the air."

A part of me had known that Valerie was going to be mad, which was why I hadn't given her any of the details beforehand. But I'd learned long ago that it was better to ask for forgiveness than to ask for permission. And besides, no way would I have thought she'd be this angry.

"It's the research team that dug all that stuff up," I said.

"Yeah, but after I told *you* about it," she replied.

I shrugged. "Well, I thought you told me so that I could use it."

"I told you because I thought you were my friend and

friends share stuff without having to worry about getting stabbed in the back."

I had to figure out how to play this because she was really upset. A tear had actually begun trickling down her cheek. And between my tutoring and her assistance at work, Valerie had been a big help to me and I didn't need her slacking off.

"What's the big deal? You don't even like Sheridan Matthews."

Valerie wiped the tears from her face. "That's not the point. The point is, I trusted you."

I rolled my eyes. *Oh, good grief.* Why was she being such a baby? "Look, Valerie. I'm sorry I violated your confidence. I didn't know it was supposed to be this big secret. Besides, I knew you didn't like Sheridan and I didn't think it was that big of a deal."

"Did you ever stop to think about me? What kind of trouble I could get in?"

Not really, I wanted to say, but I remained silent.

"You have no idea what you've done," she said, her voice taking on an eerie calm.

"Look, I said I was sorry. And on the real, it's not often that I give an apology to anyone."

She just stared at me, a hurt expression on her face, silent tears streaming down her face, before turning and walking away.

I debated going after her, not just because I was kinda sorry, but also because I had a calculus test coming up and I didn't need her mad at me. But before I could make up my mind, Dexter had grabbed my arm.

"Come on, I need to get you into the conference room. *Entertainment Tonight* wants to interview you."

"*ET?*" I asked in shock. "Like in the national show, *Entertainment Tonight?*"

"That's right, *our competition*. You know you're doing well when the competition wants to interview you," he said, his voice full of pride.

"Wow, I said, quickly pushing aside thoughts of Valerie, Sheridan, and anyone else. This was my chance at stardom, and I was about to seize it and never let it go.

Chapter 30

Between interviews, meetings, and everybody under the sun wanting more details on the Glenda Matthews story, it had been a long day and I just wanted to get home and rest. I'd known that it would be only a matter of time before Sheridan started blowing up my phone and she'd done just that. I deleted all the messages she left without listening because I was sure she was just cursing me out a hundred different ways.

I had already started planning. I was definitely playing sick tomorrow and skipping school. It wasn't that I was scared of Sheridan, but I wasn't a fool. No way would I face Sheridan's wrath so soon. I'm sure Ms. Matthews had disappeared to some exotic island to hide from the madness.

I wrapped my plush robe around me and headed downstairs. I had showered and covered myself in my favorite bath products, and I was heading to the kitchen to get something to drink. My parents were at some charity event and Sui had the night off. Most people would've been scared alone in a house this big, but not me. I relished the peace and quiet.

I grabbed a bottle of Fiji water and decided to watch television on our seventy-two-inch in the theater room since my parents only had a forty-two-inch TV in my room. My dad claimed it was excessive to get anything any bigger. Yet, he had a sixty-inch flat screen in his room. Whatever.

I began flipping through the channels and stopped on the channel that displayed our security cameras. Was that someone outside our gate? I leaned in and looked closely at the screen. It *was* someone out there! They were just standing there staring at the gate like they were trying to figure out a way to get inside. I couldn't make out his or her face or features. The figure stood there wearing all black—black jeans, black combat boots, and a black hoodie. I couldn't tell if his or her face was covered with something, but this was way too creepy for me.

I didn't immediately get scared because we did have a big iron gate around our home. Besides, it was probably just Sheridan trying to come confront me. But then I noticed the person—I couldn't tell if it was a male or female—was a lot heavier than Sheridan. When the shadowy figure began pulling at the gate, my heart started racing. Sheridan wouldn't have even attempted to do that. She knew there was no way around that twelve-foot iron gate. Plus, she would've just rung the intercom until someone let her in.

But if it wasn't Sheridan, who was it?

"May I help you?" I said into the intercom.

The figure stopped, but kept their back to the camera.

"What do you want?" I asked.

Still silence.

"I'm calling the cops," I said.

The figure stood for a few seconds, then darted off down the street.

My heart rate still hadn't returned to its normal pace. I

took a deep breath and stood up, backing away from the intercom. I felt like I was a character in one of those creepy low-budget horror movies.

I raced to the phone to call our security company. But I stopped mid-dial. What if my parents freaked out? My dad was already uneasy after the cheer story. He would surely trip over this and possibly try to make me quit.

"It was probably nothing," I muttered as I placed the phone back on the base.

Besides, I took comfort in knowing the iron gate stood between me and that freak. I double-checked the alarm, made sure all the doors were locked and headed upstairs to the theater room.

It was probably just someone at the wrong house, I thought. Or maybe it was someone trying to scare me. As I took off down the hall I thought back to the three stories I had done so far. I knew people were mad at me over the stories I'd done, but would someone seriously show up at my house trying to scare me? Didn't they fear being caught? By the time I made it to the theater room, I was back to thinking the person outside had something to do with one of those.

"There was no way I could have let the cheer escorts go!" I muttered as I entered the theater room. I found the dimmer and made the lights brighter. Once I selected the movie I wanted to see, I pressed a few buttons, started the movie, then dimmed the lights again.

I knew this film was cheesy, but I liked it and when I needed time to think, I'd zone out in front of it. As the massive screen lit up my mind went back to the shadowy figure. Who was I kidding? I could try to tell myself that was someone at the wrong house. But I knew better. The way that figure had stood staring at the camera. That was someone trying to scare me.

But who?

I thought about all the people involved in all the major stories I'd done so far—from the cheer escorts story, to the story on Sheridan's mom, to the Bling Ring. Someone was definitely trying to scare me. I don't know if they were mad about my stories or what. But they needed to know they were wasting their time, because Maya Morgan refused to be intimidated.

Chapter 31

The sound of a garbage truck outside actually jolted me out of my sleep. I looked around the theater and noticed the screen was dark. I couldn't tell what time it was because the room was always so dark, day and night.

I eased my body up from the sofa, stretched, and then yawned.

When I grabbed my cell phone I was stunned to see it was 6:30 in the morning! I had no idea when I had dozed off the night before.

Instinct made me turn on the TV and check the security camera, but the only thing I saw was my neighbor jogging.

Sui knocked on the theater door just as I was about to grab the handle and walk out.

"Will you be having breakfast before school?" she asked.

"Not today. I just need a quick shower. Where's Mom and Dad?"

"Your father has already gone in for an early meeting. Your mother is sleeping and asked not to be disturbed."

"Of course she did," I muttered. I made my way back to my room, where I showered and changed as quickly as possible, which was an hour and a half, which made me late for school—again.

I made it to school right before second period. I felt the strange vibe the instant I stepped on campus. I passed huddles of people who stood in the halls and talked about something. I didn't pay much attention to what was going on, until I arrived at my homeroom and realized class hadn't started yet.

"Did you hear what happened yesterday?" one of my classmates asked.

I whipped around because I hadn't realized someone else was in the room.

"What are you talking about?"

"Four cheerleaders were arrested! Last night at a cheer competition. Everyone is talking about it," she said.

I couldn't remember her name, and the way she looked told me we didn't run in the same circles. She had that gothic thing going, black hair, thick black eyeliner, black lipstick, and black fingernails.

"That piece you did on the cheerleaders was off the chain, but between that, the Bling Ring, and that blockbuster story on your BFF, you causing some major drama, girl," she said.

I didn't even respond. I turned around and tried to focus on nothing in particular in my notebook.

"So that's what everyone was talking about," I muttered to myself.

When the teacher walked in and barely spoke to me, I frowned. I looked around the room. I felt like everyone was looking at me crazy.

What if I was being paranoid?

So what if no one said hi to me as I walked the halls? I'd come out of the womb being fabulous, so I was used to the hate.

I had no idea what the teacher was talking about in class. I just watched the clock, waiting for the bell to ring.

It was the same thing pretty much the rest of the day—everyone acting like I was the one hooking up with men for money and making the school look bad. I don't think I'd ever been so happy to see the end of a school day.

The final bell had barely rung when I darted out to the parking lot where my car was parked.

I stopped when I saw Bali leaning against my car. I thought about taking off and running in the opposite direction because Bali put the cr in crazy. It was only because he seemed somewhat calm, standing there by my car, his hands tucked in his pockets, that I kept walking over to him.

"What's up, Bali?" I said, staying several feet away from him just in case he let loose.

"I guess your ratings are up, huh, Maya? That's what's most important, right? That you show the world how fabulous you are."

The way he was talking actually scared me. He was so calm and even-toned.

"Yeah, well, it is what it is," I replied.

He let out a small laugh. "It is what it is, huh? Who cares who is hurt in the process."

"Look, Bali," I finally said. "I hate that it had to come down to all of this. I mean, you and I were really cool."

"Yeah, until you decided to stab me in the back," he said, nonchalantly.

I tried not to roll my eyes. We'd never see eye to eye on this so there was no use trying to talk about it.

"You know when you do people dirty, it's just a matter of time before you get a taste of your own medicine," he said.

I was so sick of people threatening me. "Look, if you think you can scare me—"

Bali closed his fingers in a "shut your mouth" gesture.

"Girl, slow your roll," he snapped. "Ain't nobody trying to scare you. I'm just telling you the truth."

"Well, thank you for your version of the truth. But you can keep your predictions to yourself. If that's what you're out here getting butt prints on my car for, you're wasting your time."

He shook his head pitifully. "Nah, I was just coming to tell you I hope you're happy. Your little story, whether you did it for ratings or revenge, has ruined my life. It was the last straw for my dad and he's sending me back to Cuba."

That made my mouth drop open. Bali was always talking about how bad things were in Cuba and how he'd rather die than return there.

"What? Why?"

"*Why?* Your stupid story, Maya. Why do you think?"

I was stunned. Never in a million years would I have imagined that. "B-But you weren't, I mean, I didn't say anything about you in my story."

"You didn't have to," he replied. "We both know I was the one filming, so I was there. And when everybody is facing major trouble, they get to singing. So, yeah, you didn't mention me, but I don't know why you didn't think police would find out I was involved. So, of course, they questioned me and my dad. And of course, I denied it to the end so the cops really couldn't do anything. But guess what, my dad could. So, he's sending me back to Cuba because I have become so 'corrupted in America,' as he said."

I felt awful. Just the way he was talking, I felt so sorry for Bali. He'd told me time and time again how hard it was to be the gay son of a diplomat in Cuba. He hated even going back to visit. I couldn't imagine him living there permanently.

"Bali, I'm really sorry," I said. "I never meant—"

"Whatever, Maya," he said, cutting me off. "Just wanted to give you a heads-up. You win. This round." He stood up and started walking off. "But like I said, payback ain't pretty. And it always appears when you least expect it. Just something to think about."

He gave me the most hateful glare, before he turned and walked away.

Chapter 32

I was running late for work because Mrs. Watson and her stupid make-up class had kept me longer than normal. I had just parked my car and was making my way around the sidewalk of the building when I heard what sounded like crying and loud angry voices.

I couldn't make out what was being said or who was mad, but I knew for sure it was an argument and it was going down. I eased a little closer, making sure I was out of sight. It wasn't that I was being nosey—oh, who was I kidding? Yes, I was. That was my job.

I leaned in so I could hear better. I couldn't believe it. Was that Valerie yelling through her tears? Who in the world would be going off on Valerie of all people? She was meek and on the quiet side. I couldn't even imagine what she'd done to make anyone so mad. The way this person was yelling, I had no idea why Valerie would subject herself to being screamed at either.

"All I know is you better handle it!" a woman said.

I peeked around the corner so I could get a good look. The woman, whose back was facing me, spoke in a threatening voice. Valerie's eyes shifted to me and that's when the

woman spun around. She was still very angry. Her eyes were
fired up and her chest was heaving up and down. Her nostrils
were also still flaring. I recognized her immediately as the
woman from the picture on Valerie's key ring. It was her
mother.

"Uh, hi," I said, walking slowly

I walked slowly toward them. I didn't miss how Valerie
lowered her head and tried to dry her eyes. That was so lame
for her mom to be putting her on blast like that all out in
public.

"Hi, I'm Maya Morgan." I stretched out my hand for her
mom to shake it, but she looked down at my hand then back
up at me. She didn't smile and didn't bother to touch me.

Well, okay, then.

"I looked at that video you needed. It's on your desk if
you need to see it for yourself," Valerie finally said to me. She
spoke to me, but her voice was shaky and I felt like she was
trying to get rid of me. Suddenly, a car door opened and an
older man stepped out. I immediately recognized the gray
hair from Valerie's photo as her father. The man didn't speak
as he walked toward us. He leaned in and whispered something in Valerie's mother's ear and her entire body began to
shake. She closed her eyes and took a deep breath.

The man pulled her into his arms and held her for what
felt like forever. Valerie stood there looking down at the
ground.

I knew it would be wrong of me to start asking questions
about the stories and interviews Valerie was supposed to set
up, but I was trying to figure out what was going on.

Valerie finally glanced up and I saw the confused look on
her face. I didn't know if that was a plea for help or if she was
simply embarrassed. I had never met her parents before and I
was certain that she didn't like the way her mom had just left
me hanging like that.

I tried to communicate with her using only my eyes, but realized that she and I weren't close enough to be able to swap vibes like that.

"So we can move forward with that story then?" I asked.

"I'll be inside in a minute," Valerie said, like she was dismissing me.

"Oh, okay," I said. The look on her face—like she was terrified or something—had me a little concerned. What if her parents were abusive? What if they were threatening her?

"Oh, well," I said, heading to the door. I wasn't about to take a lick for her, but I could call the cops if something went down.

I eased inside the door and made tapping noises like I was walking off, but I tiptoed back so that I could spy on them through the vent.

"What do you want me to do?" Valerie whined.

"You need to handle this, and I mean it," her mother said, waving a finger in her direction.

Okay, that was my second time hearing her say that. Handle what? I wondered whether I should ask Valerie what was going on or wait to see if she'd say anything when she came back inside.

After about ten minutes, Valerie finally walked into the office and I jumped right in.

"Okay, what was that about?" I asked.

Valerie blew a frustrated breath, but tried to act casual about it. "My parents are trippin'."

"No kidding. But about what?"

"Look, I don't want to talk about it." She started going through some papers on the desk, trying to look busy.

"Well, if they're coming all up on the job trippin' on you, it's obviously something major. I think I deserve to know what's going on because, remember, I'm the reason you're working here. The last thing I need is for word about that little disturbance getting back to Tamara and I can't take up for you." I folded my arms to let her know I wasn't moving until she came clean.

Valerie sighed, then seemed like she was thinking. I guess she was trying to decide whether she should tell me anything. "My mom is just trippin' because—" She paused. "Because Jenn's mom is all mad at me for telling you about Sheridan's mom." She sounded like she was rushing her words out. "Jenn's mom and my mom are friends so everybody is upset with me because I told you and you did that stupid story and now the whole world is digging into it. Jenn's mom is scared she's going to lose her job. It's just a total nightmare."

"Dang." I truly didn't want all that drama popping off. I mean, I wanted the story, but I didn't want her catching any kind of grief behind it. I was about to tell Valerie that when Tamara's assistant poked her head in my dressing room.

"Hey, Maya, they're waiting on you in the studio," she said hurriedly.

"I'm coming." I looked back at Valerie. I was going to have to wait on playing Dr. Phil. "Well, I gotta go. You gon' be all right?" I asked her as I headed toward the door.

She released a pained laugh. "Yeah, you go do you."

I didn't know what that was supposed to mean and honestly, I wasn't about to figure it out. I'd wasted enough of my energy on Valerie and her family. If that's all it was, her mom was mad about my story, then she needed to get in line. Everybody was mad. But oh well, I wasn't about to sweat it. I planned to take Valerie's advice and keep doing me.

Chapter 33

I inhaled deeply, then opened the classroom door. The last few days had been nothing but stress and I needed a day at home to decompress. That had given me a reprieve from facing Sheridan, but I knew I couldn't keep hiding. I knew that I wouldn't be able to avoid Sheridan any longer. Rumor had it that she'd been looking for me for the past two days. She'd called my phone several times and left all kinds of crazy, threatening messages. She called so much that I had to block her number. Even then, she started using other people's phones. I needed to change my number, but I was too important to be starting from scratch with a new cell phone number. Besides, it wasn't like not being able to reach me by phone had kept her away. She'd even come by the house and screamed outside like some kind of crazy person. I had to send security to get rid of her.

But I knew I couldn't keep hiding out, so I entered the room with my head held high, ignoring the people cutting their eyes at me and looking at me with disgust. They could hate all day. I didn't care. I was back on top and these trolls couldn't take it.

I felt like I was safe because our teacher, Mrs. Eugene, was at the front, writing on the chalkboard. But no sooner had I sat down than Mrs. Eugene stepped outside to stop a passing teacher.

The door had barely closed before Sheridan made her way over to my desk.

"I should beat you down right now," she said, glaring at me.

I ignored her and opened my history book.

"Do you hear me?"

"Yeah, I hear you. But we both know you're all talk," I said, not looking up.

She took a step toward me, but Chenoa jumped up, grabbed her arm, and pulled her back. "Sheridan, chill. You don't need to be getting in trouble for beating down this skank."

"Yeah, Sheridan, chill. Your flunky has a point. I'd hate for you to miss the homecoming dance because you've been expelled."

Her hands went to her hips. "Is that what this is about? You want to get revenge and make up lies about my mom because you're mad because I took your man?" she said.

"Please," I laughed. "If you're into sloppy seconds, more power to you."

She took a deep breath, like she was going to try a different approach.

"I can't believe you would do something like that." She sounded really hurt. "I mean, I know we were fighting, but you took it there."

So now she really wanted to play the I'm-so-betrayed card? Give me a freakin' break. "*I* took it there?" I said, looking at her like she'd lost her last working brain cell. "You're the one that stole Bryce's phone and sent out that picture!"

"So that gives you reason to just make up lies?"

I definitely took note of how she didn't deny it this time.

"Look, don't be mad at me. I just report the news."

"That's not news," Sheridan snapped. "That stupid show you do is nothing but gossip and rumors."

I shrugged. "Then, just like I told your friends, if it's not true, why are you getting all worked up?"

She leaned over my desk, trying to look all tough. I didn't flinch. Unlike Shay, Sheridan didn't scare me. "Oh, you best believe my mom is livid. She's talking with her attorney right now."

Was that supposed to scare me? "And? The station has attorneys, too."

"She's just mad because you dropped her as your BFF," Chenoa said, pulling her arm again.

"Please," I replied. "Sheridan did me a favor. And you know what I think your problem is?" I said, looking Sheridan dead in the eyes. "You wish you could be me."

Sheridan glared at me like she wanted to kill me with her bare hands. She had moved closer to my desk just as Mrs. Eugene walked back into the room. "Ladies, I need you to have a seat."

Sheridan leaned in and whispered. "You messed with the wrong one. Believe that," she said. "You know firsthand what I'm capable of. I promise you will regret the day you ever uttered my name."

"Whatever, Sheridan," I said, as she rolled her eyes and went back to her seat. If I had a dime for everyone who had threatened me lately, I'd be even richer than I was.

Valerie came in, muttered an apology for being late, and slid into a desk in the back. I expected her to take a seat next to me, but she sat at the back of the class without even looking my way.

What's up with that? I knew she wasn't still mad about me telling her secret. I'd apologized so she needed to get over it.

I glanced back at her and she also just glared before lowering her head.

Man, screw her, too. If Valerie wanted to be mad, then so be it. I was sick of everyone at this stupid school. I had a new life and I was counting down the days until I could put this old one behind me.

Chapter 34

I was surprised to look up in the mirror and see Valerie standing in the doorway to my dressing room. Her eyes were puffy like she'd spent days crying. I hadn't expected her to come to work today since she'd been acting funny about me spilling her secret and then her parents had been trippin' with her so much.

"Do you need my help today?" she said. The way she was talking, I could definitely tell she was still a little salty. I just wasn't getting why she was still so freakin' upset.

"Look, I'm sorry," I said, swiveling around in my chair. We needed to end this pity party right here, right now. "I wasn't trying to violate your trust. I thought you disliked Sheridan as much as me so I didn't think it was that big of a deal."

"I do dislike her." Valerie blew out a frustrated breath. "It's just . . . never mind."

I wasn't going to baby her, so I took that to be an apology and moved on. "I'm glad we cleared that up," I said, turning back around to the mirror to finish checking out my makeup. "If only you knew what I've been through the past few days. Some stalker is hanging out at my house."

Valerie didn't look as concerned as I would've liked, but she did say, "Really?"

"Yeah. Then I'm getting crazy texts. They keep saying that I need to stop airing this story. Only I don't know what story they're talking about." I ran my hands through my hair to fluff out my curls. "It could be anybody. Chenoa and her friends threatened me. Sheridan threatened me. So did Evian and Bali, so I have no clue."

"Wow. Sounds like you're making a lot of enemies with this show," she said.

I shrugged. "Yeah, I wasn't trying to become hated, but it is what it is."

"You're not scared?" she asked.

Even if I was, I sure wasn't about to let her know. "Honey, Maya Morgan doesn't scare easily."

She softened her tone. "Maybe it is too much. Maybe you should let the show go."

I spun around and looked at her like she was crazy. Was she starting to hate on me, too? "Um, yeah, that's not going to be an option."

She looked like she was thinking for a moment, then added, "What about doing just the celebrity entertainment stuff? Leave all the dirt-digging stuff alone."

"Even if I wanted to do that, the producers want the dirt and so that doesn't leave me any choice."

Valerie shook her head. "I don't know. If I were you, I'd just let it go. You're going to make the wrong person angry and I would hate to see something happen to you because of that."

We were interrupted by Tamara's assistant. "Mrs. Collins needs to see you in her office," the girl said.

"Let me go. About that advice—" I stood. "Yeah, I'm good. But thanks anyway."

I didn't give her time to reply as I left. I used to think Valerie was in my corner, but she was for real tripping. But then, she probably was just mad about me "betraying her trust," you know, since we were BFFs and all now. Not.

I shook away thoughts of Valerie. She could get over it or get to steppin'.

Chapter 35

Dear Maya, I hope you die in a car crash.

I read the text message for the umpteenth time. It was the third one like that this week. Seriously? These people were going way overboard. I thought about deleting it, but decided against it. For now, I closed out the program on my iPhone.

"Hey, Sandy," I said.

Sandy rolled her eyes her eyes and kept walking.

Oh, so I guess I was going to get the cold shoulder now from everybody. Whatever. The countdown was on to graduation, so they could come at me crazy all they wanted. I wasn't the least bit fazed. I had an awesome interview set up with Alicia Keys tomorrow and if my classmates were trying to get to me, they needed to come a whole lot stronger than this. Quiet as it's kept, this entire school didn't have to say another word to me the rest of the school year. I was so over them hating on me.

"You know you're foul!"

I took a deep breath, contemplating whether I was even going to turn around.

"Maya!" I recognized Blake's little sister's squeaky voice. "What?" I said, finally turning to face her.

I was surprised she had taken this long to front me. I'd

heard that Blake's dad had bailed him out within minutes, so it wasn't like he even had to pay for his crime. "You hear me talking to you?"

"You know you're foul?" she repeated.

"Oh, I'm foul? Your brother is running around breaking into celebrity mansions and I'm the foul one? That's funny."

"Yeah, I didn't stutter. You're foul."

"Good-bye, Lisa," I said, turning to walk away.

"You know there's a pact." She was smiling like she was revealing some big secret. "High school is going to be very lonely for you."

"What are you talking about?" I really didn't feel like hearing her yapping, but the way Sandy and everybody else had been ignoring me made me want to know what was going on.

Lisa folded her arms across her chest. "Have you noticed that no one has said a word to you?" she said with a smirk. It was third period and I did notice that the only people who had talked to me in any of the classes were the teachers.

"Okay, and?"

"And that's the way it's going to be from now on." She seemed like she was taking pleasure in delivering that message.

"And I repeat, *and*?"

"Yeah, you can try to act all big and bad, but we'll see how you feel when nobody has anything to say to you."

"I'll feel just fine." I turned to walk away. So now, the whole school was playing juvenile games.

I saw Valerie later, right before I walked into my seventh period. "So, are you in this pact not to talk to me, too?"

"No, of course not," she said.

I wasn't going to point out how she'd all but avoided me all day long. I didn't know if it was because of the pact or something else had happened.

"You know I really don't care about some stupid pact."

"That's what I told everybody," Valerie said.

I stood in silence for a minute, then said, "So they're try-ing to get you in on it?"

"Yeah, but I'm cool. I didn't have many friends before, so it's no biggie," she said with a laugh.

Wow, so they hated me that much? "Well, whatever."

"Look, everyone is just mad at the whole Bling Ring, cheer stuff," Valerie said.

"How are they mad at me? They need to be mad at those thieves."

She smiled like she wanted to say something more. In-stead, she just said, "I gotta get to my last class."

I couldn't believe I was bothered by all of this so I pulled out my cell, ducked in the stairwell, and called Tamara.

"So, they're giving you the whole silent treatment?" Tamara said once I'd filled her in. "Boy, I don't miss high school." She actually sounded like she thought all of this was funny. "Well, the Drake concert is next week. I guarantee you, if anyone is hating on you, they'll quickly get over it the minute Drake takes the stage."

I heard what she was saying, but for some reason, I felt like things were going to get a whole lot worse before they got better.

Chapter 36

This was the life! That's all I could think as I took the last of my packages and put them in the trunk of my car. I'd been shopping all day and the great thing was, I hadn't spent a dime. Tamara had actually given me her station credit card and told me to go buy some new clothes. She actually gave me permission to use five thousand dollars. I would've preferred ten, but I took what I could.

My phone rang and the caller ID showed the number from the TV station.

"Hello," I said, answering.

"Hey, Maya, it's Vicki from the research department."

"Hey, Vicki," I said. "How are you?"

"I'm fine. Sorry to bother you on your day off, but I need to verify what month you said that original Bling Ring break-in happened. I'm trying to pull the police report. They might be tied to another break-in at the mansion of the head coach for the Miami Dolphins."

I wanted to tell her that they didn't need to check a police report. The Bling Ring was definitely responsible for that, according to Bali. But since that one hadn't been caught on tape, I kept my mouth closed.

I gave Vicki the info. That's one thing I loved about the research team. They were on it, so I'd let her do what she did.

I hung up, dropped my phone back into my purse, closed the trunk of my car, and walked back around to the front.

"Well, well, well. Can I go with you?"

I looked up to see two thuggish-looking guys in saggy pants. One of them had long dreadlocks and a tattoo on his neck that said KILLER. The other wore a black hoodie and had eyebrows that seemed to make one long hairy line across his forehead.

"Excuse me," I said, stepping around them.

"Killer" jumped in front of me to block my path. "Why you gotta act like that?"

" 'Cause she's one of them uppity chicks," the unibrow guy said.

"Excuse me, I really need to go." I pushed him to the side. I guess my adrenaline was up because I pushed him harder than I had expected and he immediately grabbed a fistful of my hair.

I screamed, but he didn't care. "Oh, you the type of chick that likes putting hands on a dude? I guess you like it rough!"

"Killer" slammed me up against the car. My heart raced as visions of me getting raped and beaten and left to die in the parking lot flashed before my eyes.

Where in the world was security when you needed them?

My fear seemed to calm him down. "Ummph, you a fine young thang," he said, running his bony hand along my thigh and up my skirt.

"Get off me," I said, finding the strength to push him again. He stumbled back but didn't let go of me.

"Ooh, and a feisty one," he said.

"Please," I begged as he tightened his grip on me. "Don't hurt me. I don't have any money."

The other guy snatched my Louis Vuitton. "Let me see. Shoot, this purse itself gotta be worth a couple of hundred."

Idiot. That was a custom-made, patent leather Louis Vuitton that had cost my dad six grand. Needless to say, I wasn't trying to boast about that right now.

He reached in and grabbed my wallet, then pulled out two one-hundred-dollar bills. "I thought you said you didn't have any money."

"I . . . I . . ."

"You're a liar," Killer said, squeezing my arm tightly. "An uppity liar. And me and my boy here, we like to teach uppity liars a little lesson."

"Yeah, maybe then they'll learn to keep their mouths closed and stop running around telling people's business," the other guy said.

My eyes widened in shock.

"Yeah, that's right," Killer continued.

"I'm gonna keep this money." He stuffed my two hundred dollars into his pocket. "As a service fee. But let me make this clear. You have diarrhea of the mouth and it's time for you to shut your trap."

A thousand questions ran through my mind. Were they serious? Or was this a coincidence? I couldn't believe someone would actually hire these guys to rough me up.

Killer loosened his grip, then ran his sloppy tongue up the side of my cheek. "You're lucky I'm in a hurry because I sure would like to get a taste of you."

I felt like I was going to throw up, but I was so relieved when he released me. I fell back against my car.

"Come on, man, let's go," Unibrow said.

Killer blew me a kiss as he followed his friend. He pointed a thick, stubby finger at me. "Remember, you've been warned."

They laughed as they disappeared among a row of cars.

I knew I needed to get up and go find security, but I was too scared to move. And all I could hear were the words, "You've been warned," and my gut told me that wasn't a threat. It was a promise.

Chapter 37

I watched my parents sit at the breakfast table in their usual position—my dad sipped coffee and buried his head behind the newspaper and my mom thumbed through one of her many fashion magazines. They both were fully dressed—as if they'd come to breakfast any other way.

They finally looked up and noticed me.

"Good morning, sweetheart," my dad said.

"Hey," I said. I walked in slowly and sat at the table. Sui appeared out of nowhere (she had a way of staying out of sight just enough to show up when needed) and set a glass full of orange juice down in front of me.

Dad was back behind the paper.

"Hi, honey," my mom said. Then her radar must've gone off because she narrowed her eyes at me. "Are you okay?"

I so wanted to tell them about the attack yesterday. But I'd tossed and turned all night, trying to decide if I should tell them what happened. But my mom would blow a gasket and I couldn't chance her trying to make me quit my job. I knew this was getting serious though. I could no longer pretend that this was just someone from school trying to scare me. Still, my gut wouldn't let me say anything—yet.

"Yeah, Mom, I'm fine. Why you ask?" I shrugged off her question like it was the craziest thing ever.

My dad lowered his paper. "You look . . . upset," he said. My mom smiled.

"I bet it's about Bryce," she said.

"Eeewww, um why would I be upset about that?" I asked.

"Breakups are never easy, sweetheart," my mother said, patting my hand. "But believe me, you'll heal."

I hated when she tried to get all mushy and hypersensitive with me. I didn't want to talk about Bryce, not because it hurt to think about the way he had dumped me, but mostly because I didn't want my parents to know I had lied. They had no clue that it was Bryce and not me who had broken things off. I still secretly held on to my vow to make him regret that move.

But I had told my parents that I'd called it quits with him, and hoped they'd never find out it had actually been the other way around. They didn't need to know all of the details; all they needed to know was that he and I were no longer together.

"You know, sweetie, my first love was a boy named Charles Swanson. You know, the movie director?" my mother said.

I rolled my eyes. Of course, I knew. She only told me every other day. I was just surprised she was saying it in front of my dad. But he didn't seem fazed. Probably because while Charles Swanson was an award-winning director, he was also on his third very public divorce.

"Mom . . ." I said, cutting her off before she went into her speech on how my dad had stolen her away.

"Sweetheart, it's obvious Maya doesn't want to talk about her breakup," my dad said, going back to his paper. "She's focused her priorities on more important things. Which is the smart thing to do, if I must say so myself."

My mom paused, studying me. "You sure you're okay?" she asked me again.

"Mom, I'm good." I frowned. "I'm, like, loving life right about now. I mean, why do you keep asking?"

"Oh, honey, it seems like something's on your mind. I'm just checking, making sure everything is okay. You have anyone interesting on your show?" Mom asked.

I was gulping down the orange juice when she asked about the show. But that was just the break I needed. I was thrilled she had changed the subject. If we talked about the show, I wouldn't have to worry about her digging too deep and pulling out of me what had happened last night, or anything else about Bryce.

"OMG! I am so hyped." I grinned.

Instantly, my mother's eyes began to twinkle. She smiled and looked at me like an eager puppy, a cute one, but a puppy nonetheless. I put the glass of juice down and started in about the interview.

"Drake is coming to do a concert on campus and it's all everyone can talk about," I said. "And then, I have an interview with Nicki Minaj this week!" Tamara had shared that bit of news yesterday after I'd called her just before I went to bed.

I hoped the excitement in my voice would be enough to keep her off the Bryce topic. I watched as my mother's perfect eyebrows bunched together and she tilted her head slightly.

"Nicki Minaj?" she asked.

I sighed dramatically, and rolled my eyes.

"Mom! Please. Do. Not. Tell. Me. You don't know who Nicki Minaj is," I said, and rolled my eyes again. This time the atmosphere had changed and I was glad for the lighter mood.

My dad's newspaper collapsed and he popped his head and nose into our conversation.

"She's only the hottest female rapper around today," my dad said and stunned me to silence.

Blank stare.

I was at a complete loss for words as he tried to *school* my mom on Nicki and her music. The craziest part was he actually sounded like he knew what he was talking about.

"Some Nicki Minaj songs are pretty good, like 'Fly.' Some are just okay, like 'Moment 4 Life.' But some are not so good, like 'Super Bass,' " my dad continued.

My mouth was on the table as he talked, like he was some kind of new-school rap historian.

"It's got a good beat, but the way Nicki dresses and acts with guys, well, I don't know that it's the example I want you following. She curses in almost all of her songs. I think that's why you see so many teenagers cursing all the time—it's what their favorite celebrities do." He shrugged.

Both my mom and I were stunned. When she finally found her voice, she asked dad. "Uh, and how exactly do *you* know so much about this hot female rapper?"

"Well, when you have a teenage daughter, you make it your business to know these things," my dad said. He smiled in my direction, but I was still in a state of shock.

Clearly I had been underestimating him. If you would've told me that my dad not only knew who Nicki Minaj was, but could also rate her songs, I would've called you a bold-faced liar! My dad had no way of knowing how many cool points he had earned with me this morning.

"Besides, Nicki is a client." He smiled.

"Of course," my mother said, seemingly relieved that my dad wasn't leading some kind of secret double life.

My mom turned her attention back to me. "So, she's coming on the show then?"

"Yep, and she's gonna talk about her new album and movie role." I left off the part about her sharing her dirt about the beef with her manager. No need for the crazy looks from my dad.

"Yep. I'm supposed to go backstage and interview her, so everyone is stoked about it. It's all *everyone* is talking about," I said.

"This sounds so exciting. Do you know what you're gonna talk to her about?" my mom asked.

Even if she didn't mean it, I was glad she was trying.

"Well, I already know just about everything there is to know about her. I mean, I do do my homework, Mom."

By now, my dad had turned his attention back to his newspaper and I felt a bit better.

"I know you do, honey. I know you take your job seriously and I'm so glad that you've found something you enjoy after all of that drama surrounding that other program," my mom said.

I hated when she went back to that mess that had gone down with *Miami Divas*. It was so obvious, even a blind person could see, that those other girls (and Bali) had no talent whatsoever. I actually liked doing a show by myself a whole lot better.

In the past, if we all didn't agree on something on the show, it would turn into a big argument and nothing would get done. But now, once I sign off on the ideas the producer and I come up with, it's smooth sailing from there. And when it came to *Rumor Central*, that's what I needed. Smooth sailing. Between Bryce and what had happened last night, I didn't need any extra drama.

Chapter 38

I slammed my locker shut and nearly dropped the book I had just grabbed. Bryce was standing right next to my locker. He looked me dead in the eyes and didn't even try to glance away. I wanted to vanish, but I couldn't. I wanted my skin to crawl at the sight of him, even wanted to *want* to throw up in my mouth, but none of that happened. Instead, my heart started to beat all fast, like it might leap out of my chest at any moment.

I was more than mad at myself, and my heart, for the way they had betrayed me. *We* were all supposed to hate Bryce. Like, ugh-the-sight-of-your-face-makes-my-eyes-burn *hate*, but instead, I felt the stupid goose bumps that rose up all over my skin and my stomach churned like crazy.

Butterflies?

Really?

How could I still feel like all *love at first sight* after what he had done to me?

Relief finally washed over me when his teammate, Jason ran up to us.

"Hey, bro," Jason said, interrupting Bryce's stare-down. I

don't know if he was trying to send me some kind of stupid message with his eyes, but I wasn't having it.

Jason was nowhere near as hot as Bryce, but I instantly decided he'd have to do. That was the only time Bryce finally pulled his sleazy gaze away from me. It wasn't that his eyes were no longer dreamy, but when he'd decided to hook up with Sheridan everything about Bryce had suddenly become gross and instead of being the man of my dreams, he starred in my daily nightmares.

"Jas, what's clack-a-lackin'?" Bryce said.

He made me so sick with the corniness. I used to love when he tried to be cool; of course that was all a part of what had made me think he was the love of my life. But that was back in the day. This was a new day. I knew how I could make Bryce pay.

"Jason!" I cooed. "What's up, handsome?"

He looked surprised, and I was glad. I knew Bryce was extremely jealous and I wanted desperately to make him explode.

"Umm, hey, Maya," Jason stammered. He looked confused. I couldn't tell if he was surprised at my tone, or if he was trying to decide if he was going to break this whole 'silent treatment' these busters were giving me at school. It didn't matter. I was just trying to get to Bryce. And I had his attention; now I just needed his heart in a vise grip, so I could squeeze tightly. "Dang, boy," I said, admiring his biceps.

I could sense the rage that Bryce tried to hide. If Bryce was a cartoon character, smoke would have been coming from his ears right now. His eyes had always given him away. When we were together, we'd joked about how his expressions, his eyes, and his face were always a dead giveaway to what he thought.

"Whoa, what are you wearing?" I purposely leaned in and sniffed Jason's neck. I pulled back and smiled at him.

"Dial soap," Jason replied.

What an idiot!

"Dial?" I leaned in again. "Hmm, well it must mix really well with your body's scent, 'cause you smell real good, all manly like," I teased.

That fool actually grinned like he'd just won a new title. When I reached up and squeezed Jason's bicep again, Bryce looked like he wanted to pounce. His eyes literally followed as my hand moved up Jason's arm. I prayed that would be on instant replay in Bryce's head all night. Why should I be the only one who tossed and turned at night?

"You been working out?" I asked.

"Welllll," Jason dragged. He glanced between Bryce and me before he continued. "Coach does have me on this special workout plan, you know, since all these schools have been heavily recruiting me to come play football for them. Gotta do what I can to stay fine."

I wanted to puke.

"Well . . . whatever you're doing, you need to keep it up. I see a huge improvement," I said.

"Really?" The shock in Jason's voice was almost laugh-out-loud funny, but I held it together. I caught a glimpse of Bryce out the side of my eye and cheered on the inside. He was beyond furious.

"Really, Maya?" Bryce slowly said.

I allowed my eyes to roll up and down Bryce's body; then I frowned, and turned my attention back to Jason. I moved away from Bryce and was now all up in Jason's personal space.

"So, with you looking and smelling all good, I think I'm, like, really feeling you," I said.

Jason's eyes grew so big, I thought they might pop out of their sockets. I wasn't sure whose were the biggest though, because Bryce shook his head like he was trying to adjust his ears to what he heard.

Instead of responding, Jason pointed at me, then back at his chest like a preschooler. I loved it!

"That's right," I said.

Both of their attentions locked on me. Bryce was all up in our conversation like I was talking to him instead of Jason. He made me so sick, I wanted to ask him where my former BFF and his new bottom-barrel chick was, but I remained focused.

"I wanted to kinda ask you something, and you don't have to say yes right now. I'm sure you probably got plans already," I began.

I dug into my Michael Kors bag and grabbed a set of tickets. I was gonna give them away during a student body rally, but I decided this was as good a time as any to start making *new* friends.

When their eyes fixed on the Nicki Minaj tickets and backstage passes, both of their mouths dropped open.

"Are those what I think they are?"

"Only if you think they are Nicki Minaj concert tickets and backstage passes," I said.

"Ah." Jason scratched above his eye, and shifted his weight to his left side. He suddenly seemed nervous, like he wasn't sure what to do with his hands. "Are you really giving those to me?"

"If you want them. Nicki is also having a private party."

"Do I get to go with you?" he asked excitedly.

Bryce frowned and cleared his throat.

"What, man? You're with Sheridan now," Jason said, like he really could understand why Bryce would have a problem.

My stomach turned flips. I guess all was fair in love and war. So, if Bryce wanted to go there, two could play that game.

"That's messed up," Bryce mumbled.

Jason didn't seem fazed as he smiled at me. "So what time am I picking you up?"

"How about I have the limo come get you?"

"Oh, we're rollin' like that?" Jason smiled like he'd just won the lottery or something. "So, let me get them digits," Jason said, "so I can call you before then. Matter of fact, why don't you roll to this football party with me tonight?"

I wanted to tell him to get a freakin' grammar book, but I needed to see this plan through.

Jason looked back at Bryce. "You don't mind me bringing her to our party tonight, huh? I mean, since you'll be there with your new chick, it shouldn't be a big deal."

Our party? Oh, I was definitely going now.

Bryce huffed in disgust, then walked off.

"Yeah, you gotta excuse him," Jason said. "But he's probably kicking himself cuz everybody's talking about what a fool he was to let you go."

Really? With all the hate I was getting, I would've thought the opposite. But then again, they could front all they wanted. At the end of day, I should've known all the haters simply wished they had my life. Shoot, if I wasn't me, I'd hate me, too.

I really wasn't looking forward to hanging out with Jason, but since I wanted to make Bryce sick, I had to do what I had to do.

I rattled off my phone number and prayed that I could make it through the evening with Jason without throwing up.

Chapter 39

No one needed a break like I did. Maybe hanging with Jason wasn't going to be so bad, after all. He'd wanted to come pick me up for the party, but since I don't do Toyota Camrys (what he drove), I told him I'd just meet him there. I almost backed out until I got a text from Sheridan. She said Bryce told her about me coming and if I was smart, I'd stay home. I definitely wasn't going to let her punk me, but if I had any thought of staying home, once Kennedi saw that text, that thought went out the window.

"No, this trick didn't," said Kennedi when I filled her in on what happened. She'd come up from Orlando for the weekend for her cousin's wedding, but she'd ended up hanging out with me.

"Whatever, you know I'm not messed up about Sheridan."

"No, I know you're not about let her scare you," Kennedi said, getting up and heading to my closet. "Gimme fifteen minutes and I'll be ready to go."

I laughed because I knew with Kennedi, that fifteen was definitely going to be thirty. Normally, I wouldn't be messed up about some high school party, especially since I was rolling with real celebrities now, but my desire to stick it to Bryce was enough to make me want to be there in full effect. And full effect I was. I was wearing a Maxima one-shoulder short jumper. It cut high enough on my thighs to make any guy drool and it was low enough not to be slutty. Kennedi was looking just as fierce in a fire red tank top and sequined shorts. We were both more than ready to let our hair down and hang out.

When I turned my car onto the street there was no doubt I was in the right place. Trucks and cars lined both sides, which made the street even more narrow.

By the time I drove to the end of the street and turned the corner, there was not a single spot in sight.

"Okay, I can't believe they don't have valet," Kennedi griped.

I ignored her as I pulled into someone's driveway and turned around. The best I could do was go back to the entrance of the subdivision and try to look for a spot back there.

"At least this means the party is tight," I said.

"You're right about that. I miss this in Orlando. Those busters throw some whack parties."

"Well, I just want to have a good time," I said.

"And don't forget, stick it to Bryce in the process," she laughed. Nearly thirty minutes and two and a half blocks later, I wasn't as enthusiastic as I had been earlier. I finally found a spot I squeezed my car into and we began the trek up to the house. Along the way, people were outside. Some were drinking, and a couple was arguing. I wasn't trying to get all up in their business, but I hated when couples fought in public. We passed them up and came up on a few people who hung around the backs of two pickup trucks. It was like they were having their own party.

None of those faces looked familiar to me, so I walked until I arrived at the front lawn of the house party. Two girls were there dancing with each other and a small crowd of guys had formed around them.

The guys yelled all kinds of stuff at them, and they kept moving and touching all over each other.

"Freaks," Kennedi muttered as we squeezed past the crowd of rowdy guys and moved our way up the walkway.

The closer we got to the front door, the louder and harder the music pumped. It was a wild scene. People were all over the place, in the lawn, in the garage, and hanging out of cars in the middle of the street. I knew the neighbors in this upscale neighborhood were having a fit and it was probably only a matter of time before the cops showed up and shut this joint down.

There was no point in trying to knock or ring a doorbell at the front door. The music was so loud, it seemed to rattle the house.

I eased the door open in case someone was on the other side. A rainbow of colored lights danced around the packed room. Bodies were sandwiched against each other in the middle of the massive living room, and other people lounged on chairs and couches or stood and held up the walls. Nearly everyone in the room had either red plastic cups or beer bottles in hand as they swayed or moved to the ear-thumping music.

"I know doggone well this isn't Kennedi Harrell?"

We both turned to the voice coming up from behind us and were shocked to see Kennedi's ex, Sean. Sean was the only guy that could make Kennedi weak at the knees. He went to a different school on the other side of town, so I never saw him, but I knew for a fact that Kennedi never got him out of her system.

"What's up, Sean?" she asked.

"I can't believe you were in town and didn't call me."

She shrugged. "Just came down today to hang out with my girl."

He finally noticed me and said, "What's up, Maya?"

"Nothing much."

Her barely gave me time to finish before he turned back to Kennedi. "Can I holla at you outside?"

Kennedi looked over at me. I know she wanted to go so I just said, "It's cool, I'll just see you inside."

She looked relieved as Sean took her hand and led her away.

I walked inside, where I nudged this girl, Cecily, and was about to lean in to ask her a question when she jumped back and frowned at me.

"Hey, I just wanted to know if you'd seen Jason," I said.

She rolled her eyes at me and the girl next to her did the same. Then they both frowned at me like I had offensive body odor. Whatever.

Maybe it was because I was sober in a room full of people who had been drinking, popping pills, and who knew what else, but suddenly as I passed people and made eye contact I began to feel strange.

Had she rolled her eyes at me, too?

Was he looking at me like I'd stolen something?

As I passed, some people even turned their backs on me.

By the time I made it into the kitchen, it was obvious that stupid silent treatment had carried over to this party.

"Charles, where's . . ."

I didn't get to finish my question before he lit into me.

"Why are you even here, man?" he asked. His boys stood behind him, nodding in agreement. "Haven't you heard, snitches get stitches?"

Really?

"She's meeting Jason," someone said. "I just heard him tell someone that he's only giving her the time of day so he can meet Nicki Minaj."

I was stunned. Jason was a scholarship student so he was

lucky I was even giving him the time of day. I looked around at the blank faces that stared back at me.

Suddenly, my tongue felt like it had instantly doubled in size. I couldn't get it to move and form words that made sense. I looked around the packed kitchen, and noticed even the people huddled near the keg stopped to look at me.

I looked around the room and everyone looked at me like I was worse than the dirt beneath their sneakers.

That was bad, but what was even worse was who stumbled into the kitchen and stopped suddenly at the sight of me. Evian, Shay, and Sheridan exchanged glances. "Somebody should've told me this party was open to riffraff," Shay said, staring me up and down.

I couldn't believe Shay's hood behind was talking about me of all people being riffraff.

"What's *she* doing here?" Evian said.

Was *she* me?

I swallowed the massive dry lump in my throat and backed away from the group with the keg.

"Whatever!" I said. I thought of darting out of there, but I wasn't about to give them the satisfaction.

I dug into a trash can and pulled out a can of coke. I shrugged as every eye in the room watched my every move. If they thought staring at me was going to do something I had news for them.

After I grabbed the soda, I found a paper towel, wiped it dry, then snatched a handful of popcorn and eased past Sheridan, Evian, Shay, and Bryce.

Who needed all those idiots anyway?

I eased my way out to the backyard, where once again, the moment my presence was noticed, everyone stopped whatever they had been doing.

I sighed and rolled my eyes.

"Heeeeey, Maya, whasup?" Jason said, making his way

through the crowd and over to me. He stumbled and caught some girl's arm to keep himself from falling.

"My bad," he laughed, trying to stand up.

I couldn't believe this fool was sloppy drunk already. He'd known I was coming—you'd think he'd try to stay sober until I got there.

"Come here, girl," he said, grabbing for me. "Gimme a kish."

Ewwww. He was slurring his words. I stepped aside and this time, he actually fell to the floor. I looked up and saw Bryce and Sheridan standing against the door staring at us. How was I supposed to make Bryce jealous when this idiot Jason was stupid drunk?

"Ooooh, baby, youuuu. You got what I want," Jason started singing from the floor.

Several people were laughing like that was really funny. I was so utterly disgusted.

Shay eased up on the side of me. "Yeah, I can see how Bryce would be sick over you kicking it with him. He's a class act." Everyone around Bryce burst out laughing.

"Whatever," I said, turning to leave out of the kitchen. As soon as I spun around, someone actually pushed me and I ended up falling—right on top of Jason. The room erupted in laughter. I had never been more embarrassed in my life, especially when Jason grabbed me and started trying to kiss me right there on the floor.

I managed to pull myself up, while everyone continued laughing. I no longer cared who said what. I just knew that I needed to get out of there and get out now! I went to find Kennedi and tell her this party was definitely over!

Chapter 40

I was really and truly fed up. The people at school hated me. The administration hated me. Everyone was talking about suing me. And worst of all, some idiot was terrorizing me via email and text. Throw in that disaster of a party last night and this had turned into more than I'd bargained for.

That's why I was standing in Tamara's office with the difficult decision that had kept me up, tossing and turning all night long. I just couldn't do this anymore.

"So, what's going on? You got some more juicy gossip for us?" Tamara asked.

I sighed. "No, I'm all gossiped out."

She lost her smile as I continued. I didn't sit because I just wanted to get this over with. "Tamara, you know I love this job. I love what I do. But I can't do this. Someone is stalking me." I decided against telling her how all the hate was really getting to me. I knew that wouldn't move her. But maybe she'd listen if I told her I was in danger.

She shrugged like it was no big deal. "Please, that's par for the course. But don't worry, I'll alert security."

I sighed. I'd decided not to tell anyone about the attack at the mall because I didn't want people thinking I couldn't handle this job. But I no longer had a choice.

"I was attacked the other day. Two guys roughed me up and told me to shut up and stop digging into other people's business."

Tamara folded her arms on her desk. "I'm sure they were just trying to scare you."

The way she was just blowing me off was making me so mad. "They warned me to stop with the show. It's just too much. I want out."

She leaned back in her chair and folded her arms across her chest. "So the money, the fame. You just want to walk away from it all?"

Of course, I didn't want to walk away from that. But at the same time, I simply didn't know what else to do. I didn't scare easily, but between those thugs at the mall and the constant drama, I was fed up.

"Look, I understand your concern," she continued. "And I know you wanted us to beef up security, and we actually have a bodyguard for you starting next week."

Oh, so *now* they got the bodyguard.

"We'll have your mail filtered," she continued.

"Tamara, I'm just tired of all the drama," I replied.

"Look," Tamara said, sitting up. "You're in the big leagues now so I'm gonna need you to be a big girl. Do you know how much hate mail Oprah has gotten in her lifetime? What is it you and your friends say? If you don't have people hating on you, you're not doing your job."

"But this is more than that," I protested. "I don't want to do this anymore. I quit."

She stood up and started gathering papers on her desk. "I would love to sit and discuss this with you, but I have an executive meeting I need to get to and you need to get in with Ken and talk about next week's show."

I hated that she was just blowing me off. "What if I just quit?"

She stopped, stood and stared at me for a minute, then without saying a word reached into her file cabinet. She pulled out a stack of legal-sized papers and handed it to me. I took it and looked at it.

"What's this?" I asked.

"That is your contract," she replied.

"Oh."

"And what does the duration of that contract say?" She tapped the paper.

I read the spot she pointed to. "Two years."

"And how far are we into that contract?"

"Two months, but . . ."

"But that means, for the next twenty-two months, you're not going anywhere unless I say you're going somewhere. You signed off, your attorney signed off, your parents signed off. So as far as I'm concerned, there's nothing to discuss."

Was she for real trying to get tough with me?

"Oh, I can pay your little funky money back," I quickly said, reaching for my purse.

"Oh, the money isn't the issue," she replied. "Not only would we sue for breach of contract, but I will have you and your family tied up in court for so long your little trust fund will be gone."

I just stared at her in disbelief.

"But, since I'm sure you'll make the right decision, we won't have to worry about that, now will we?" She didn't wait for me to reply. "Ken's waiting on you," she said over her shoulder as she walked out the room.

Chapter 41

I didn't even want to get out of bed. It wasn't that I was that distraught over having to continue the show; it was that I couldn't stand people trying to boss me around. And yes, Tamara was my boss, but I still wasn't having it. I'd made up my mind that I was going to talk to my dad when he got home. He was going to have to help me figure a way out of this job.

I was waiting on him when he got in that evening. He looked at me and could immediately tell something was wrong. "Hey, sweet pea," he said. "What's going on?"

"Nothing," I said, meekly. I hadn't figured out yet how exactly to present my case.

He removed his jacket. "Now, you know I know better. What's wrong?" he repeated.

"I'm tired. It's like everybody at school hates me." I decided to start there, then ease into the stalking part because he would be furious that I was just now saying something.

"Since when do you care about someone hating?" he said, smiling.

"I don't, really." I shrugged. "I don't know."

"I think you're a little frustrated right now. And while I

don't exactly approve of all the gossip, you're making a name for yourself. Some of the interns at the office were talking about you at the water cooler yesterday."

I cocked my head. My dad's office was definitely upscale. "Really? Why didn't you tell me?"

My dad shrugged. "I'm telling you now." He grabbed his briefcase, opened it, and started ruffling through some papers. "But I support whatever you want to do. Although I don't believe in quitting. Morgans aren't quitters. We see things through to the end, no matter how difficult."

I sighed. That was my dad's motto for everything. When I wanted to quit ballet, he wouldn't let me. The same went for violin, French lessons, and every other thing I'd ever done.

I heard my cell phone ring and used that as my excuse to bail. "Let me get that." I quickly left the room and raced into the den, where my cell phone was.

I groaned when I saw Tamara's cell phone number, but went ahead and pressed ANSWER anyway.

"Hey, how are you?" she asked.

"Fine," I said, curtly.

"Look," Tamara said, "Maya, you know how much I like you and I apologize for being so blunt earlier. But you caught me at a bad time. I'd been putting out fires all day and just was in a foul mood. You don't know how much I had to fight to get you all the perks you wanted, then you wanted to turn and bail on me."

"I didn't want to bail on you," I said, falling back on our leather sofa. "I just . . . I don't know, all of this is just getting to me."

"Why? You said yourself you aren't friends with these people anymore. You're on the verge of superstardom and the show has done so well in the ratings there are talks of taking it syndicated."

"What does that mean?"

"That means we'd take it national," Tamara said.

This was my first time hearing this. "You mean I would air in more than Miami?"

"Yes,ma'am, you'd be airing all over the country. Maybe the world. It's not a done deal yet, but it's looking real good."

I hoped she wasn't just saying something to keep me from being mad. But then, Tamara had always been about the business. "Wow," I said, as visions of Emmys, Grammys, and MTV Awards flashed through my mind.

"But that good news isn't actually why I was calling. I was actually calling to tell you . . . are you ready for this?"

"What?"

"You know all the drama Usher was going through in his custody battle? He wants to talk to you about it."

"Are you freakin' kidding me? How does Usher even know about me?"

"I told you, Maya. You may be local, but your name is already spreading across the country. He rarely does interviews. His audience is young women and he wanted a platform that he knew wouldn't bombard him. And he's here filming a movie. Our people got with his people and they want you to come on set to film him. That is, of course, if you still work for us."

Me. *And Usher?* Oh my, God! Sheridan absolutely loved Usher. She would die a slow death at the thought of me getting to interview him.

Forget everything I'd been feeling earlier. "Oh, I definitely still work for you."

"So you're no longer bummed about the job."

"Yeah, I'll get over it," I said, laughing. "Usher can make a girl get over anything."

Tamara laughed with me. "That's my Maya. Oh, and just so you know, everything is set for the Drake concert at your school. Just another reason you can't go anywhere."

"And on that note, I gotta go. I got to call Davion, the girl who does my eyebrows, and my stylist. I have to be on point for this interview."

"Well, Maya that won't be hard because you're always on point."

"Thanks, Tamara."

I hung up the phone. My attitude had done a one-eighty and I was excited beyond belief.

Chapter 42

I leaned in and checked my appearance in the bathroom mirror. My eyes were puffy and red. I guessed that's what a late night of partying with celebrities would get you.

After my interview with Usher, he'd invited me to a private party and I'd kicked it all night long. I hadn't gotten home until almost three in the morning. Good thing my parents were sound sleepers and they hadn't heard me come in. It was difficult because this balancing both worlds was kicking my butt. I'd actually started counting down the months until graduation, and trying to figure out how I was going to break it to my parents that that whole college thing they'd been planning for me wasn't going to happen. Everything was on hold for *Rumor Central*. I knew they were going to trip, but I really didn't see what the big deal was, especially since the whole reason people went to college was so that they could make money, and I was definitely making money.

I looked at my watch. Valerie was running late. She was supposed to meet me in here five minutes ago. She'd been acting funky ever since my story. She really needed to get over it or I was going to have to look at replacing her.

I was just about to text Valerie when the door swung

open. "Here you go," she said, handing me my English homework.

"Thanks for doing this," I said, deciding not to fuss about her being late. "There's no way I could've gotten this done without you."

"How was the party?"

"It was awesome." I was just about to go into all the fabulous details when I noticed the look on her face. She'd actually come to the interview, but she hadn't been invited to the after-party. I hadn't really thought it was a big deal because she's not about that life, but she still didn't seem her usual self.

"What's wrong with you?"

I hoped she wasn't about to tell me that she was upset about the party.

"Oh, just the same drama," she said.

I suppose at that point I probably should've asked her more details, but I really didn't care. I just needed this homework.

"So, are you sure everything on here is right?" I asked.

"Yeah, the stuff is a breeze."

"See, that's why I had you do it. I probably would still be working on it," I said.

"So, any updates on the Sheridan story?" Valerie asked.

"Still working on it," I said with a smile. "I'm going to find that kid if it's the last thing I do."

"How do you even know Glenda's child is even alive?" Her question caught me off-guard. This was the first real conversation she'd had with me in a while.

"Maybe she's not, but I at least want to get a picture." I tucked my homework in my bag.

"Why are you so gung ho on this?"

I turned to face her. "Because I need to knock little Sheridan and her mom off their high horses."

"Maybe you should just leave it alone." I know she wanted to say something about the trouble she was getting into behind the story. But shoot, the damage had already been done. There was no sense in me bailing on the story now.

"Maybe you should just stick to English homework," I replied. Debbie Downer needed to go somewhere with all that negativity.

"I'm just saying, this isn't about me. I mean, Glenda Matthews is pretty powerful."

"And yeah, so is Maya Morgan," I reminded her. "And whose side are you on anyway?"

"All I was trying to say is that you said yourself that you were getting tired of all the dirt and gossip."

"I was, but I've suddenly been rejuvenated."

I was tired of talking to her. For a minute, I'd found myself really liking her. But now, Valerie was really starting to work my nerves.

Chapter 43

This should be one of the biggest days of my high school career. I mean, all that hate was gone out the window. Well, except for my former crew. My classmates were jocking me like the superstar that I was and I was about to go on stage to introduce Drake. I'd taken pictures, done interviews, and everything, and now I was about to go on and introduce him. But I was so nervous, I could barely think straight.

One text had ruined all of my excitement.

U think ur cute. We'll see how u look w/blood splattered all over that peach jumpsuit. #udietoday

The fact that I was wearing a peach jumpsuit meant the stalker was right here. But in a sea of people I had no idea who it could be.

All of this had me completely shook up. This wasn't a game anymore. I'd made the wrong people mad. It had to be Evian and her people, or I wouldn't put it past Sheridan's mom to hire someone. But then again, Chenoa and Blake were pretty mad.

"Uggh," I muttered. I used to think it was cute being hated, but now I didn't even know where to zero in to find out who it was that was making my life a living nightmare.

Pow!

I screamed as I dropped the mic and dove to the floor. "Dang, you a'ight?" one of the stagehands asked.

I looked up nervously, my eyes darting around as I wondered why no one else was taking cover.

"Get down, get down," I hissed. "Someone's shooting."

He looked at me like I was crazy. "Ugh, no. A light bulb burst," he said, pointing up to one of the lights on the ceiling.

Several of the technical people started laughing as I tried to regain my composure and stand up.

"Sorry, I—I guess I'm a little nervous."

"My grandmother used to always say if you scare easily, you ain't living right." He laughed.

I wanted to tell him nobody asked him about his stupid grandmother. My look must've told him I didn't see anything funny because he turned and scurried away.

"Maya?" Tamara said, putting her hand on my shoulder, causing me to jump again. "What's wrong with you?" she asked, looking at me strangely.

"All this noise and people sneaking up on me. It's just too much," I snapped before I knew it.

"Whoa. Take a deep breath, chill out."

I inhaled, then exhaled. "Sorry. Just a little stressed." I wanted to tell her about the text, but my mom was standing right behind her and if I uttered a word about a stalker, my mom would march me right up out of there and not let me continue. And since that wasn't an option, I just remained quiet.

"So, what's going on? Are you ready?"

"Yes," I said, looking out over the audience. "Let's just get this over with."

Chapter 44

Okay, enough was enough. I'd gone from thinking there was something wrong with Valerie to having no doubt.

This chick had just rolled her eyes at me.

I turned my back on her, but suddenly whipped around and I could've sworn she was mocking me with her hands behind my back.

I was mortified and hot at the same time. I frowned and my eyes narrowed. It was obvious I must've been boring her. We had only been talking about an idea for the show. And it was her job to listen to me and take part in our brainstorming session. But she had an attitude and this time, wasn't trying to hide it.

"You done yet?" she asked dryly. She even twisted her neck when she asked the question. And to think, I'd just got through defending this trick. Word about her parents tripping had gotten back to Tamara, who'd asked me about it. After I'd come to Valerie's defense, Tamara had said, "You sound like you're best friends with the girl, the way you're taking up for her."

"Never that," I replied. "I just feel sorry for her sometimes. She's such an outcast and I know she just wants to be me. But overall, she's all right, especially because she does my homework without complaining."

Valerie had popped up in my dressing room just moments after that conversation. Maybe she'd overheard me. Maybe that was why she was standing here giving me bonafide attitude. Seriously, she acted like she could've been doing anything else in the world but working with me.

It wasn't that I needed her to hang on my every word, but she made me feel like I was wasting *her* time.

"What's going on with you?" I asked.

My tone softened and I even adjusted my thoughts about the attitude she had been dishing my way. Maybe she was worked up about something else, something entirely unrelated to me and the job we had to do.

"What are you talking about?" she snapped.

It wasn't the question she asked, but *how* she asked it that really rubbed me the wrong way again. She had more attitude than I had seen in quite a while, and I couldn't remember a time when I'd seen it coming from *her* of all people. I wasn't sure what to make of it.

"Do you have something else you need to be doing right now?" I asked. This time though, I threw just as much attitude back as she had thrown to me.

Her hands went to her hips, her face twisted, and I could've sworn she sucked her teeth.

"What's that supposed to mean, Maya?"

Even the way she said my name sounded like I'd stolen her boyfriend (as if her lame behind could even get one). This was ridiculous. It seemed like every day the number of people who were mad at me, didn't like me, or tried to kill me with their eyes, grew.

The last thing I needed was Valerie of all people jumping on that bandwagon, too. The rest of the entire student body had that covered. But, Valerie and I *had* to work very closely together. If drama jumped off between *us*, I'd really have issues. Without her, I'd really be struggling. I could admit that.

With that in mind, I did a mental check and readjusted my tone and my attitude—again. Maybe Valerie was fighting with her parents again. I had no clue what was wrong with her, but I knew I needed her to get it right. The way she had talked to me and the way she was acting were not good. And this was the only pass she was going to get.

"Seems like you're mad or something," I said. "I'm trying to figure out whether we can finish taking care of ideas for the show, or if you want, we can try to do this later."

When I said it, there was not a hint of attitude in my voice. But her body language made me feel like she still had major beef with me.

"I'm fine," she said, but she sounded fake. "So are you any closer to figuring out who was stalking you?" That seemed to come out of nowhere.

"No, but I'm sure it's Sheridan or it may even be Bali." I hadn't heard from Bali directly since his father withdrew him from school, but I had been getting these hang-ups from some anonymous number that could have easily been him. "Or, it could even be one of the people I did a story on," I added, even though I was no longer sure.

The door opened and for a change, I was glad for the distraction, or at least I thought I was until my eyes fixed on Jennifer Graham.

"Umm, what's going on in here?" she said.

Jennifer, Valerie's friend, looked back and forth between the two of us after she asked her question. I knew she wasn't expecting an answer from me. I had barely said two words to her our entire time in high school. And if Valerie was mad at me, I was double sure that she was, too.

"I told you to wait 'til I call," Valerie said to Jenn before I could respond or react.

"Yeah, but that was like almost two hours ago. How was I supposed to know you still wanted me to wait?"

Valerie rolled her eyes again. I wasn't used to all of this attitude coming from her. But I fell back and let those two go at it.

The two of them exchanged awkward glances and I suddenly felt like I was out of place.

"I told you I'll let you know when I'm done," Valerie insisted.

She spoke to Jenn through gritted teeth. All of a sudden, Jenn's entire demeanor changed.

"Well, when you didn't call, I didn't know what to think," Jenn tried to explain. "How was I supposed to know you guys weren't done yet?" She shrugged.

"Go back and I'll call you, like I said," Valerie snapped.

My eyes grew wide as I watched the two of them. It was something about the way Jennifer acted that caused an alarm to go off. It wasn't just that she had an attitude with me, too. It was almost as if she was nervous around me. Like she had something to hide. Then the way she cut her eyes at me, throwing me daggers, raised a red flag. I hadn't thought about it before. Even though we'd never run in the same circle or anything, she had never been an issue to me.

But now, in my opinion everyone was suspect.

After Jennifer walked out of the room, I realized something. Outside of that one evil look, she'd never once looked me directly in the eyes. She hadn't even spoken to me. And what was all that talk about waiting on a phone call? Suddenly, my mind raced back to moments when I'd seen Jenn and Sheridan talking over the past few weeks. It was always in hushed tones, like they were conspiring together. I knew that Jenn used to tutor Sheridan, last year. But as far as I knew, she hadn't started back this year.

A thought suddenly occurred to me. Jenn hated me for getting her mom in trouble behind the Glenda Matthews story. Sheridan hated me for doing the Glenda Matthews story. If anyone had motive and would want to shut me up, it would be those two!

That would also explain why all of a sudden, Valerie was throwing major attitude my way.

It had finally started to make sense to me. What if Valerie had found out what Jenn was doing and she was trying to gauge my temperature to figure out what I knew? I couldn't imagine that she would be in on it, but I could definitely see her trying to help her girl out.

I thought about trying to feel Valerie out, but she seemed even less interested than before Jenn had walked into the room.

"You know what, we don't have to do this now," I said.

Valerie didn't say anything. That confirmed for me that I must've been on to something. The way I saw it, if Valerie had issues with her parents, the moment I called her on it, she would've started spilling.

But when Jenn had walked in unexpectedly, Valerie had become even more upset. The change was like day and night. There had to be something there, and I knew I'd have to find a way to get to the bottom of it.

Chapter 45

My gut was telling me I was on to something. My head, on the other hand, was telling me to leave it alone. I was sure Valerie shared my business with Jenn and I know for a fact that Jenn idolized Sheridan. I was willing to bet Jenn was passing info on to Sheridan. I wasn't one hundred percent sure, but I was determined to find out. That was why I now sat across from Valerie and Jenn at lunch.

"What?" I asked when I noticed the strange look they were both giving me. "I can't sit here?"

"No," Valerie said. "Of course you can. It's just that you're always busy during lunch."

"Yeah," Jenn said, narrowing her eyes at me. "You've never eaten with us your entire time in high school."

I shrugged. "There's a first time for everything." I turned back to Valerie. "I'm hungry. I don't have coaching today so I just came to hang out with you guys. I also wanted to tell you about the big development."

Valerie's eyes grew wide. She looked at Jenn, then back at me.

"It's cool if she knows," I said. "Everybody is about to find out anyway."

"Find out what?" Jenn said.

I took a bite of my chef's salad, then leaned in to make sure no one else could hear. I didn't care really about anyone else hearing, but this was all part of my big act.

"I have two huge stories I'm working on," I said. "We're really close to finding out who the child was that Sheridan's mom gave up for adoption." When Jenn's eyes grew wide, I knew my suspicions were right on target.

"Don't worry," I told Jenn. "This has nothing to do with your mom. We were able to find this out from somewhere else."

Jenn just glared at me, angrily.

"What? How?" Valerie said. I didn't pay her much attention. I was too busy studying Jenn's reaction. That girl was definitely hiding something.

"We have a top-notch research team," I continued watching Jenn. "They were able to dig up some documents. They're actually waiting to have them delivered. But it's just a matter of days," I said, feigning a smile. I was lying through my teeth, but I didn't know if I needed to lay a trap.

"So, yeah, we got that and some more information on the Bling Ring. We're about to do a huge exposé on them all," I added.

"Are you sure you want to do this?" Valerie asked.

"I've never been more sure," I replied. "It's my job to get to the bottom of things."

"Do they know who the child is?" Jenn asked.

"Not yet, but they will," I said, smiling. Yep, I could tell from the look on her face, she'd definitely taken the bait.

Chapter 46

Shut up or be shut up.

I stared at the note tucked underneath my windshield, my hands trembling as they held the piece of paper.

"Hey, Maya."

I groaned as Bryce approached me. It's like he wouldn't give up. I wasn't in the mood to deal with him and was definitely about to tell him so. His eyes went down to the piece of paper in my hand.

"What's that?"

"None of your business. That's what it is," I snapped.

He shrugged, then flashed that crooked smile that made my heart melt. But right about now, I had bigger things to worry about than Bryce's stupid smile.

"Sorry. I was just wondering," he said, before taking a deep breath, then rushing his words out. "I'm tired of acting like it's not killing me to be without you. And I can't stand watching all these other guys going after you."

What other guys? Jason? I hadn't talked to his buster behind since the football party (and for the record, no, I didn't go to the Nicki Minaj concert with him. If I could've taken his tickets back, I would have). I wanted to ask Bryce what in the world he was talking about, but he kept talking.

"When I saw someone putting that note on your window, I got jealous." He cracked a smile. "Thought maybe it was someone leaving you a love letter."

Under normal circumstances, I would've been flattered by his jealousy, but I couldn't focus on that right now.

"What do you mean, you saw someone putting this on my car? Who was it?"

He shrugged. "I don't know. They had a hoodie on. I was upstairs." He pointed to the classroom on the second floor. "You know how I'm always daydreaming. I was staring outside the window and I saw a person at your car."

"Was it a boy or a girl?" My heart started racing, especially because I had been in class with Sheridan, so it couldn't have been her.

He shrugged again. "I couldn't tell. They were skinny, but like I said, they had a hoodie on." He paused and studied me. "Maya, why do you look like that? What's going on?"

"Nothing," I replied. I didn't know whether to be more scared or relieved. If it was someone on campus, maybe it was a student after all, just trying to scare me, and not one of Evian's goons or someone that could cause some serious damage.

Before I could say anything else, Bryce snatched the paper from my hand.

"Stop it!" I yelled. "Gimme that. That's none of your business," I said, reaching for the paper.

He stepped out of reach, using one arm to hold me back. "Shut up or be shut up," he read.

He looked at me. "Maya, what is going on? What is this about?"

"Nothing," I said, my voice shaking.

"Don't tell me this is nothing." He shook the paper at me. "What is this about?"

My shoulders sank as I stopped trying to grab at the paper. "I don't know. Someone is messing with me. They are trying to scare me."

"Is this behind your show?"

"I don't know what it's behind and I don't care. I don't scare easily."

He glanced down again. "Maya, this is serious. Have you been to the cops?"

"For what? It's probably just some stupid classmates trying to get me all worked up." I finally managed to snatch the note back.

"And what if it's not?" he said, matter-of-factly. "I mean, I know you've made some people mad, but is it really to this point?"

"Obviously." I sighed. I wasn't about to stand here and unload on Bryce. "Forget about it, Bryce. It's not your concern."

"If it concerns you, it concerns me."

I turned my nose up. He made me so sick. And if he wasn't so dang cute . . . "Get over yourself, Bryce. We're no longer together."

"That doesn't mean I'm gonna stop caring for you." He took a step toward me.

I took a step back. "Well, you need to." I folded my arms across my chest to let him know his brown eyes, crater dimples, and jacked-up smile were not going to get to me.

"Maya, you can be mad all you want, you can go off later, but right now we need to go to the cops."

I shook off the trance I felt seeping up on me. "And say, what, Bryce?" I snapped. "Someone is sticking letters to my windshield?"

"I don't know, but you can't just let this slide. This isn't some kind of joke."

I really didn't want to talk to him about this, but Bryce was the first one who had even taken my concerns seriously.

"I don't know what you should say, but you need to say something. We can go right now."

"I'm on my way to work. I have to tape today." I was working on another blockbuster story about a Hollywood teen starlet who had been caught shoplifting in Miami. We were interviewing the security guard who had caught her. No way was I going to miss that.

"Okay, fine, then we can go tomorrow?" he said.

I stared at him like he was Boo-Boo the fool. "What part of there is no *we* are you not getting?"

"I'm not listening to you. You don't have to like me to let me go to the police station with you. This is major, Maya."

I was really feeling the fact that he was being so forceful about it. I sighed and was just about to agree when Sheridan came stomping our way.

"Bryce!" she called. "What are you doing?"

He immediately let out a groan and I was back to being mad.

I turned up my lip. "Yeah, Bryce, go see what your girl-friend wants. Don't worry about me or my problems. Just leave me alone."

"Stop it, Maya. . . ."

Sheridan stomped in his face, completely ignoring me with her back to me. "Bryce, I've been calling you. Why aren't you answering?" He looked at her and cut his eyes. She looked back at me and scowled.

I reached for my car door. "I'm gonna let you two work this out. I have more important things to do."

"Maya . . ."

I gave him the hand and he stopped midsentence. I rolled my eyes, got in the car, and drove off.

And to think, he'd almost gotten through to me. Good thing almost doesn't count.

Chapter 47

I took my time getting home because what Bryce said was weighing heavily on my mind. He was right about one thing. I couldn't keep at this by myself. I was exhausted and wanted this all to end. Not the show, but the hate, the not knowing if the threats were a harmless prank or something that I actually needed to be concerned about.

I pushed the remote to open our gate and noticed the limo parked out front.

"Oh, crap," I said. I forgot that my mom was leaving for her annual shopping trip to Italy with her girlfriends. She was going to be so mad about me getting home late.

So, even if I wanted to come clean, I couldn't because it would ruin her trip. Or, I could wait until she left, then say something to my dad. My dad would be much more level-headed about this whole thing.

I pulled into the garage, parked, and made my way inside where I saw my parents standing in the foyer looking intense. I hadn't stepped inside when the look on my mother's face told me that this conversation was not going to be pretty.

"Hey," I said slowly.

My mother spun toward me. "Do you have any idea what kind of mess you have gotten us in the middle of?"

"What now?" I asked, blowing a frustrated breath.

"Glenda Matthews is suing us for slander," my mother announced. "How could you do that awful story?"

"I was just doing my job, Mom," I replied.

"I thought Sheridan was your friend. How in the world could you turn on her like this?" Had she not been listening to anything I said lately?

"Now, Liza, calm down," my father said.

"Calm down? Not only does she have the woman threatening to sue us for everything we own, but everyone across town is talking about it!"

My father continued talking. "As I was telling you before Maya arrived, Glenda has no grounds for a lawsuit. She's just doing that for publicity's sake."

"Yeah, especially because it's true. How is she going to sue me for something that's true?" I asked.

"That's what I told your mother," my dad said. "This is all for show. She just wants the newspapers to report that she filed a lawsuit. Then, she'll drop it."

I rolled my eyes. "Well, she can't sue me anyway. She has to sue the station."

"All of that is beside the point," my mom snapped. "Whether it's thrown out or not, the last thing we need to be doing is getting tied up in court over this foolishness." She looked at my dad and shook her head. "I told you this job was nothing but trouble." She turned to me. "Maya, I want you to quit this job."

"Dadddd!" I cried.

"Liza, don't be so rash." My dad turned to face me. "But, sweetie, your mother and I are concerned. The stories that you're doing seem to be opening a Pandora's box."

"What does that mean?"

"It means that it's more trouble than it's worth," my mom

shouted. I just wanted her to go already. She massaged her temples. "Do you know that Donna is backing out of the trip because she doesn't want to be associated with the mother of a child who's causing so much havoc?"

"So is that what your concern is?"

"Of course not," my dad answered. "Your mother is just blowing off steam."

My mother took a deep breath to calm herself down. "Sweetie, your father's right. I mean, it is Donna's loss if she wants to back out. But my point is, we don't need our name dragged through the mud. Can't you find something else to do?"

"But I like my job," I protested.

My mother shook her head, then glanced at her watch. "I need to get going or I'll miss my flight." She looked at me. "Do I need to cancel my trip and stay here and help you deal with this mess?"

I was touched that she would even consider that, although I don't know if she really meant it or if she was just talking. Regardless, I said, "Of course not, Mom. The station has all of this under control. Go enjoy yourself."

"Well, I'm telling you now, when I get back, we're going to sit down and have a family meeting about this because I have a real problem with this job." She gave me a warning look before heading out the door.

I didn't say anything, but I knew right then and there, if I told her anything about a stalker, that would be the final straw. But I couldn't live my life in fear either.

"Good-bye, honey." My mom kissed me on the forehead.

My father flashed a sympathetic smile as he picked up my mom's Gucci duffel bag. "I'm going to walk your mom out."

I plopped down at one of the seats at the bar. No way could I tell my mom now, but I needed to at least tell my dad, even if I had to play it down. I would leave off the part about the thugs attacking me at the mall, because that sure enough would make him side with my mom in forcing me to quit.

"Are you okay, dumpling?" he asked when he walked back in.

"Yeah."

"Do you want to talk?"

"Not really."

He smiled, then pinched my cheek. "Everything is gonna be okay." He started to walk away when I stopped him.

"Dad?"

"Yes, hon?"

"There is something I need to talk to you about." I paused. "Obviously, I'm making people pretty mad with my reports. Well, someone is sending me threatening text messages trying to get me to stop."

He looked shocked. "Why are you just now telling me this?"

"Because it's not that big of a deal now. It's just kinda creeping me out. I don't think it's anything, but I was wondering if Daniel could go with me to file a police report tomorrow. You know, just in case."

He narrowed his eyes at me. "Just in case what?"

"You know someone put my tires on flat. I just want something in writing just in case we need to file another police report." I was so downplaying everything.

He looked at me skeptically. "Are you sure that's it?"

"I'm sure, Dad."

"Okay, I'll call Daniel and ask him to meet you downtown at the police station."

"Thanks, Dad," I said, standing up and kissing him on the cheek.

He stopped me. "Maya, are you sure about this show?"

I forced a smile. "I am. I've never been more sure of anything else." That was a bold-faced lie because I wasn't sure about anything anymore.

Chapter 48

I paced up and down the sidewalk of the Miami-Dade Police Department. Daniel was supposed to meet me at the police station this morning to file a report. But Daniel was twenty minutes late and not answering his stupid phone. I was just about to call his office again when the phone rang and my dad's number popped up.

"Hey, sweet pea," he said.

"Dad, oh my God!"

"What's wrong?"

"Daniel isn't here yet."

"That's actually what I was calling about. He just called. He got summoned back into court unexpectedly so he's going to have to reschedule."

"Reschedule! My life is in danger and he has to reschedule?"

"Honey, it couldn't be avoided. We'll do it in the morning."

I couldn't believe this. "Why can't you come?"

"Sorry, I'm actually tied up and can't get away."

"What do you mean, can't get away? I need to get this reported."

"You don't need me for that. Just go in there and file a re-port."

I couldn't believe this! My life was in danger and he couldn't get away?

He hung up before I could say another word. I couldn't believe I had to endure this. "Uggh!" I dropped my phone into my purse and headed to the police station.

Some yellow-haired old woman looked up at me like I was bothering her. "May I help you?"

Yeah, you can start by getting an attitude adjustment, I wanted to say. Instead, I just said, "Yes, I need to file a police report."

She eyeballed me before grabbing a clipboard and hand-ing it to me.

"Why do I have to do all of this? I just need to talk with someone," I said.

"Fill this out, please," she said, pushing the clipboard to-ward me again.

"Ugggh!" I snatched the clipboard then stomped off. I glanced around the dirty police station. Where in the world was I supposed to sit? This place was disgusting. I stood at the counter, quickly scribbling in the blanks, before handing the papers back to the woman. "*Now,* can I talk to someone?"

She took the clipboard and set it down.

"My dad is Myles Morgan."

The woman looked at me, unfazed. "My dad is Michael Jackson," she said with a straight face.

Oh, she had jokes. At a time like this? I didn't think so.

"Is your manager in?" I asked. I was not about waste any more time with this old hag.

Just then, an overweight man walked up.

"Hey, Shirley, what's going on?"

"Are you a manager?"

He laughed. "I'm a supervisor. This isn't Burger King."

So everybody had jokes.

"Yes, I'm trying to file a police report," I said. "My life is in danger and this thing here is acting like I'm irritating her."

The woman looked like she was about to say something, but the man put his hand on her arm. "Shirley, I'll take this." He turned to me. "Come on back."

I rolled my eyes as I stomped past her. I pulled my purse close as I walked down the long hall. Even though I was in a police station, I didn't feel safe.

Inside his grungy office, the officer motioned for me to sit down.

"Now, what is it I can do for you?" he asked.

"I'm being stalked."

He glanced down at my paperwork. "So, someone is texting you and hanging outside your house."

"And jumped me in the parking lot of the mall. It's crazy and I need something done."

He looked up at me and sarcastically said, "Maybe it's because you're so fabulous. I mean, that's what you wrote here," he said, tapping the notes section.

"That's exactly what it is," I said, without missing a beat.

He chuckled, shook his head, then said, "Ma'am, we have your report. We'll put it in the system."

"And then what? You need to investigate, call the SWAT team, make an arrest."

He set his pen down and folded his hands in front of him. "And who would you like us to arrest?"

"Whoever it is that is doing this."

"And who would that be?"

"I don't know," I snapped. "It's probably Bali Fernandez."

"Who is that?"

"A former friend. It's either him or Sheridan, or Shay or Evian."

He had the nerve to roll his eyes. "So you don't know who it is?"

"It's one of them. I'm almost sure of it."

"Where's your proof?"

"I don't have any!" He was working my nerves.

"Ma'am, we have some real crimes to solve."

"This is a real crime," I said, pounding his desk. See, if my dad had been here, they wouldn't be treating me like this.

"Well, if you don't know who we should arrest, how are we supposed to know?"

"Isn't that what I pay you for?" I snapped.

"You pay me?" He smiled. "Can I have a raise?"

"You know what I mean. My tax dollars pay you."

"Oh, you pay taxes?"

"Well, my daddy's tax dollars pay you, so technically, you work for me. And I need you to find out who this is that's stalking me."

He sighed like he was tired of dealing with me. "We'll get right on it. I'll call *CSI Miami* to see if they can investigate."

I stared at him, trying to see if he was being funny. Then it dawned on me that *CSI* was some TV show. I wasn't going to waste my time with this man. It was obvious the police weren't going to help me. And if I wanted to get to the bottom of who was attacking me, it looked like I would have to do it myself.

Chapter 49

I never had any intention of playing private eye. But it was like nobody took this stalker serious but me (and well, Bryce, but he didn't count). My dad wasn't making it a priority; the police had all but blown it and me off. So, the last thing I wanted was everyone sitting around at my funeral talking about, "I should've listened." I was going to take matters into my own hands.

My first move was to get some evidence against Jenn. Or Jenn and Sheridan. I had to sneak into the locker room.

The idea seemed pretty simple, at first. Since my gut was telling me Jennifer Graham was key to figuring out who my stalker was, and since Jenn was the student tutor for the girls' basketball team, I figured I would start there.

Over the past couple of days, I had monitored their practice schedule and decided this was the day to make my move. I was not, and had no desire to be, an athlete, so I knew it would come as a surprise to many to see me in the gym.

"You need something?" one of the coaches asked. I hadn't even seen her come up behind me. "You must be lost."

"Oh, no. I'm scouting locations for my next story," I lied. She looked at me all cockeyed, like she wanted to say something, but decided against it in the end. Ever since I'd started working at *Rumor Central*, when people saw me around campus they were guarded. It was almost like everyone was scared I'd be exposing their secret or looking for something wrong. I didn't have time to worry about her feelings, though, so I kept walking.

Once I made it down the hall a bit, I turned and saw the coach was still looking at me. I could only imagine the thoughts that ran through her mind.

Practice would be over in less than thirty minutes and I needed her to leave so I could move forward with my plan.

At the end of the hall, I stopped and knelt down near a back door. I stretched my arms out like I was trying to measure the width of the door. The coach watched me for a few minutes; then she turned and walked out of the door.

The moment I realized she was gone, I waited a couple more minutes, and then I ran back down the hall and into the locker room.

"Uuugghh!" The thick smell of musk and feet assaulted my nostrils and nearly brought tears to my eyes.

"Man, if this is what the girls' locker room smells like, I can't even imagine what the boys' locker rooms are like," I muttered. I swallowed and blinked a few times.

I only had about fifteen minutes before the place would be crowded with players and I didn't want to be caught. I glanced around and searched for anyone who might be hanging out in the locker room. Confident that I was alone for the most part, I dug into the bag that was slung across my body. I pulled out the small digital voice recorder and the packaging tape.

Once I had picked the perfect spot, I straddled the bench that was in the middle of the row of lockers. All of a sudden I heard a noise that made me go cold.

Had someone come in? By my calculation they still had a good ten minutes of practice left.

A creaking noise seemed to be getting closer and closer. I flicked the switch into the on position on the recorder and sat as still as possible and waited for someone to say something to me.

Instead, I heard what sounded like muffled music. That's when I slowly turned and realized it was the janitor. She had on a pair of headphones and she used a feather duster like a microphone. She had stopped her trash can on wheels to belt out a song in Spanish. Her eyes were closed as if she was really into whatever song she was singing. I turned and quickly reached under the bench. I tapped the recorder in place before I stood.

A few seconds later, her eyes opened and she jumped, like I had startled her. She snatched off the headphones and smiled nervously at me.

I smiled back, nodded, and scooted past her and the big trash can she had wheeled into the aisle. I kept walking and didn't look back.

Just as I made it halfway down the hall, the door from the gym burst open and a group of boisterous players came rushing through. I had made it out just in time.

Once I rushed back outside, I went to the parking lot and climbed into my car. The plan was simple, I'd wait until most of the players left the locker room; then I'd sneak back in to get the recorder.

Nearly an hour later, I still sat waiting. I was more than frustrated, but I needed to figure out what was going on.

Because of the idle time, I started to wonder whether this was really a good idea. What if someone found the recorder? What if I was caught removing it? As doubt started to settle in, I looked up and saw some action.

The players had trickled out of the locker room in pairs at first, but a few seconds later they were coming out in groups. Just like I suspected, Jenn was one of the last ones out. My heart quickened when I saw Sheridan right next to her. So it was Sheridan she was working with!I waited for them to get in their cars and leave; then I got out of my car and started walking toward the gym.

Getting back inside wasn't as easy as it had been before. I grabbed the handle on the door and it was locked! My heart sank to my feet.

"Dang! The stupid doors lock when you come out!" I mumbled.

I cupped my hands up against the glass and peered inside. The hallway was empty. Not a soul was in sight!

Just then, I saw someone walk out of the locker room and stroll toward the door. I jumped back and waited.

"Dang, you scared me," she said the moment I popped out to catch the door when she walked out.

"Sorry," I said and quickly dashed inside.

This time, I moved with authority, like I belonged there. Once I was inside again, I couldn't remember which row! I hadn't counted. I started looking at names and after walking the third row, I found the bench.

I straddled the bench, eased my hand underneath, and plucked my recorder.

I switched the off button and ran up out of the gym. I kept running until I made it back outside and to my car.

Chapter 50

I couldn't wait to get home and listen to the tape. I just knew that it would hold the key to helping me figure out who was behind all my drama.

Since I was too anxious to wait, I pulled into the Starbucks parking lot next to our school, whipped out the recorder, and pressed play. At first, there was nothing but crackling sounds and people laughing as they filed in and out of the locker room. Then I heard it. Sheridan's voice.

"So, did you do it?"

"I did what you asked me to," the other person said, sounding irritated.

I strained a little to make out the other voice.

"Look, if it's a problem—" Sheridan said.

"It's not a problem. I did it, okay?"

Okay, now I was sure. That was definitely Jenn. I knew I was on to something!

"Then why are you trippin'?" Sheridan asked.

"I just don't like this."

"It's almost over."

"I just don't feel right about it."

"Okay, just do this one last thing for me and I won't ask you anymore."

"That's what you said the last time," Jenn said. "I'm sorry, Sheridan. I'm done."

Sheridan huffed. "So, it's like that?"

"Yeah. You're on your own now."

"What am I supposed to do?"

"I don't know, but I can't help you anymore."

The tape grew silent, except for the sound of someone walking away. Then, Sheridan screamed, "Ugggh!" before hitting what sounded like a locker.

I fell back in my seat. I was happy that my suspicions had been confirmed, but frustrated because I knew that wouldn't be enough for police. I needed Sheridan to confess to actually doing something, to admit to being behind the stalking. Based on what I had right now, all of my sneaking around had been for nothing!

I tossed the recorder down, ready to give up. But just as quickly as that thought came, I pushed it away.

No, I would have to figure out another way.

My cell phone rang and I looked down to see Bryce's number pop up. I almost didn't answer, but I was frustrated and who better to unleash on than Bryce.

"What do you want?" I said, answering.

"You."

"Please, Bryce. Your little girlfriend may buy your game, but I don't," I snapped as I started my car back up.

"It's not a game. She's not my girlfriend. And I wish you would stop saying that."

"I wish a lot of things, Bryce," I said softly. I didn't mean for my attitude to up and leave, but it took off on its own.

"Look," he said. "I just wanted to know what happened with the police."

"None of your business."

"You might as well let me help you because I'm not giving up."

I was so frustrated I wanted to cry. And it took a lot to make me cry. "You probably just want me to stop doing the show, too. Hey, for all I know, you're the stalker," I couldn't help but add.

He let out a small laugh. "Yeah, I'm stalking you, but I'm not sneakin' and doin' it. I want you back and I'm not trying to hide. I don't care who knows it."

That made me smile and I was actually glad he couldn't see me. "Whatever, Bryce."

"Where are you going?"

I paused as I thought about what he was saying. "How do you know I'm *going* anywhere?" I looked around the parking lot.

"Uh, I don't know," he stammered. "It just sounds like you're in your car."

I relaxed a little. My paranoia was getting to me. "Don't worry about where I'm going. Matter of fact, don't worry about me. I'll work all of this out and it's nothing you need to be concerned about."

He sighed. "Okay, Maya. But I'm here if you need my help."

I rolled my eyes. "Don't worry. I don't need your help. Not now, not ever." I hung up the phone and pulled out into traffic.

Chapter 51

I had just pulled on to Interstate 95 when I glanced up into my rearview mirror and saw a white car speeding toward me. I looked down, then back up because the car didn't look like it was going to stop.

The car actually pulled up behind me and tapped my bumper. My heart dropped as I grabbed the wheel to try and keep from losing control. I quickly darted over to the exit and the white Ford Taurus did the same.

Oh my God! I thought. They were trying to run me off the road.

I pressed the OnStar emergency button.

"911, what's your emergency?"

"Someone is following me," I screamed. "They're trying to run me off the expressway."

"Ma'am, where are you?" the dispatcher asked.

The car rammed into me again. I screamed as I struggled to keep from careening off the freeway.

"Ma'am, where are you?" he repeated.

"I don't know." I glanced up at the large green sign on the highway. "I'm exiting near Pembroke Park off of Interstate 95."

The car swerved and followed me through the exit.

"Can you see the person following you?" the dispatcher asked.

"The only thing I can see is the person is wearing some kind of hoodie." The hooded stalker was back. And this time, I felt like he wasn't trying to just scare me. He was trying to kill me.

"Ma'am, can you get to a safe place?"

"If I could get to a safe place, I'd be at a safe place!" I screamed.

"Okay, ma'am, I need you to calm down."

Suddenly, another pair of lights came speeding on the side of the white car, honking and flashing its lights, so the driver sped off. I tried to get a license plate number, but I was too worked up to read the plate. I was shocked to see the Mustang whip in front of me as Bryce rolled down the window and waved for me to stop. I pulled over to the shoulder. I had never been so happy to see someone.

I couldn't think as I opened my car door and all but fell into his arms.

"Are you okay?" he asked.

I found myself shaking uncontrollably.

"It's okay, it's okay," he said, stroking my back. "The police are on their way."

"I couldn't even tell them where I was," I said.

"Don't worry, I called them when I first noticed him hit you."

That made me stop and back away. "You were following me?"

"I'm sorry. I was really worried about you. I've been trailing you since you left the school."

Okay, this was really creepy. "Whatever, Bryce. Leave me alone." I had pulled myself together, somewhat.

"Look, I just wanted to know if you went to the police."

"Why are you worried about me?" Truthfully, I was acting mad, but I was so incredibly grateful that he had been following me. Who knew what would have happened if he hadn't been?

A car sped by, honking at us, probably because Bryce had parked so crazily on the shoulder. He pulled me farther from the street so I wouldn't be in any danger.

"I'm sorry for freaking you out. But I could tell from the other day, this stalker had you more worried that you were letting on. So yes, I am following you. Someone is stalking you and you continue to blow them off. This is crazy. What happened when you went to the police?"

I sighed, then, desperate for someone to talk to about this, finally decided to stop fighting him. "They're not trying to be any kind of help."

"Are you kidding me?" he asked in disbelief.

I nodded. "I'm just going to have to figure out who's doing this on my own."

"How are you going to do that?"

"I don't know."

"So who do you think it is?" he asked.

"It's somebody from school, I'm sure of it. But I just don't see how one of them would try to kill me."

He pulled me toward him. This time, I didn't fight him. "Well, I tell you what, we're going to figure this out if it's the last thing we do."

"We?" I said softly.

"Yeah, we." He took my chin and lifted it so I could look him in the eye. "Maya, I messed up and I'm sorry. I should've never listened to Sheridan and I definitely shouldn't have just broken things off with you like that. Let me help you, please?"

I wanted to go off on him, tell him what he and Sheridan could do, but I was tired. I was tired of trying to figure this out on my own. I was tired of being an outcast. And to be perfectly honest, it just felt good to have him hug me. It felt good to have someone back in my corner. I didn't say a word, but the way I buried my head in his chest must've given him all the reply he needed.

Chapter 52

If you had told me two months ago that I would be working with Bryce Logan in any shape, form or fashion, I would've told you that you must've been smoking something. Yet, here I was, trying to come up with some kind of master plan to track down a stalker.

Bryce and I were sitting at the table in his den. I didn't want to meet at my house because I didn't want my mom calling the house phone and asking a million questions.

We'd actually written down all the names of people I thought could be my stalker on Post-it notes and laid them out across the table.

I noticed Bryce's phone light up and Sheridan's picture popped up. I immediately felt myself getting mad. But he pressed IGNORE and kept talking.

"So, which of these do you think it is?" he asked. There were about ten names, everyone from Evian to Chenoa to Blake. But Sheridan's name sat at the top of the list and I just knew it was her. I just needed to figure out a way to prove it.

"If I knew who it was, I wouldn't need you here," I snapped.

He had the nerve to look like I was hurting his feelings. "Look, I'm just trying to help."

I sighed. If I wanted his help, I knew I needed to stop being nasty. For the most part, I had been cool, but every now and then I would slip and let a little anger creep up.

"Okay, fine." I circled Sheridan's name on the paper. "I'm sure it's your girlfriend." He cut his eyes at me and I flashed a weak, apologetic smile. "I think it's Sheridan."

"I just think we're looking in the wrong place," he said doubtfully.

Now, he was really making me mad. "If you're gonna be taking up for her, I will need to just leave."

"I'm not trying to take up for Sheridan, but I just don't see her doing something like that."

"Are you going to help me or not?"

"Of course I am. I want to know who's doing this to you just as bad as you do." He sighed like he didn't want to fight. "So, what do you need me to do?"

I'd thought about how trying to tape Jenn and Sheridan had been a bust, but I still felt like she was key to cracking this thing.

"Okay, I'm going to skip fourth period tomorrow," I said, referring to the one class I had with everyone—Bryce, Sheridan, Valerie, Jenn, and all of my former friends. I want you to tell Sheridan I'm not there because we found her mom's kid and I'm preparing some big story or something."

Bryce looked unsure. "This sounds dangerous, Maya, because if it really is Sheridan, then she'll obviously go to any lengths to get back at you. I mean, do you really think Sheridan is capable of murder?"

I shook my head. "I don't know. I used to not think Sheridan was capable of a whole lot of things, but something is telling me it's her. But I have to catch whoever it is."

"So, what's the plan?"

"You tell Sheridan that I'm at our family's Miami Beach house. That's where the person is going to meet me with details and proof to back up the story."

"Maya, I don't like this. What if it's not Sheridan?" He tapped one of the Post-it notes. "What if it's one of Evian's goons? You know she's connected to the mob. Those people don't play."

"Bryce, I don't need you to fight me on this."

He gave a resigned sigh. "Okay, fine."

I was so glad that he decided not to keep fighting me. "My guess is once you tell her, if she's behind all of this, either she or Jennifer will head my way to try and stop me."

He looked at me like I'd lost my mind. And maybe I had. I was just tired of living in fear and wanted to bring an end to this.

"It will be okay, really," I said. "You just have to follow her. Once she gets there, I'll have a camera set up and rolling. We'll catch her on tape."

"I don't like this."

"You don't have to like it. Just do it."

He glared at me before finally saying, "All right, Maya. And what if it's not Sheridan?"

"Then no one will show up at the beach house," I replied. "But it is her." I cocked my head since I could tell he wasn't going to let it go. "But if it's not, we'll come up with another plan."

Chapter 53

I had been a nervous wreck all day long. But I had a good feeling that this was all about to be over. In fact, I'd called Tamara on my way here and without going into details told her I'd have a blockbuster story for her tomorrow. It was my hope to have proof of the Miami socialite who was stalking and terrorizing me.

I'd set up video cameras all around the beach house and I was ready for Sheridan to show up. I figured if she tried to disguise herself, not only would Bryce catch her, but everything would be caught on tape. If she hired someone, that person would be caught as well. And I could take that to the police. They'd have no choice but to listen to me then.

Bryce had called me to tell me everything was going as planned. He told me Sheridan had asked a hundred and one questions. He said even nosy Valerie had jumped into the conversation, asking questions. I could tell by the tone of his voice that he was starting to think maybe Sheridan *was* behind everything.

My phone rang and I saw Bryce's number and immediately picked up. "Hey, how's it going?"

"So far, so good."

"Are you with her now?" I asked.

"I'm trailing her. She was really upset after I told her. I'm not sure if she's coming there, but she left campus about twenty minutes ago."

"Can she see you?"

"I'm in my brother's car. She won't recognize it." Bryce uttered a curse word, then said, "She's driving like a freaking maniac. It's obvious she's upset."

"Bryce, is she heading my way?" My heart started racing in anticipation. I was so ready to confront her. If I had been thinking, I would've had a camera operator there and everything so I could do a story revealing Sheridan as the stalker.

"I can't tell if she's coming toward the beach house. She's turning to get off the freeway."

"Just follow her." I scurried around, double-checking the camera. The last thing I needed was Sheridan's confessing everything and us not catching it on tape.

"Okay, this looks like this may be a bust," Bryce finally said, interrupting my thoughts. "She's turning into the mall."

"*The mall?*" I asked. Okay, this wasn't adding up. If she knows I'm about to meet my source, and she's the stalker, why in the world would she be at the mall?

"She's going inside," Bryce said hurriedly. "I'm going to follow her in."

"Okay, just let me know." I hung up the phone, frustrated. This whole plan was falling apart. Maybe Sheridan wasn't the stalker after all.

I waited for about thirty minutes, pacing back and forth, trying to figure out what I was going to do if Sheridan didn't take my bait. I knew she shopped when she was upset, so that would explain the trip to the mall. But if she was gunning for me, stopping to shop didn't make sense.

The phone rang again. I saw it was Bryce and immediately picked up. "What's happening now?"

"Okay, I'm not sure what's going on, but she just got a phone call and it has her crying. Now she's rushing out of the mall."

"Where are you?"

"I'm in the car, following her. I think she may be coming your way. I heard her say, 'I'm goin' to Maya's now.' "

Oh my God! She was really about to come confront me. "Okay, I'll have everything ready," I said.

No sooner had I hung up the phone than I heard a sound coming from the kitchen. I stopped, fear gripping me. Sheridan couldn't possibly be here yet.

"Who's in there?" I called out.

If I'd been thinking straight, I'd have known that was a pretty dumb question because what killer ever says, 'It's me'?

Silence filled the beach house. Maybe this wasn't such a good idea after all. Sheridan I could handle. Some other goon? I didn't think so. I quickly gathered my things and was about to hightail it out of there. I had just reached for the door when I heard, "Leaving so soon?"

I turned around to the figure wearing the black hoodie, pulled down low and swallowing her frame. I squinted and leaned in toward her. "Valerie?"

She laughed. One of those crazy, evil laughs. "That's right, it's me."

"What are you doing here?" I said. "How do you even know about this place?"

She walked and ran her fingers along the back of the sofa. "Oh, I know a lot that you don't give me credit for."

Something about the crazed look in her eyes made me extremely nervous. This was some major weirdness right here.

"Did you follow me here?" I asked.

"Yes, because I want to be you so bad that I follow you around. Isn't that what you told Tamara?"

So she *had* overheard me. I looked at her, confused. "So, is that what this is about? You're mad about something you overheard? You know I was just running off at the mouth."

"Yeah, you do a lot of that," Valerie said. "You run off at the mouth. You take secrets that were meant for your own ears and you tell the whole world, just so you can come up!"

Oh, she was for real tripping. She was actually still mad about that? "So, that's what this is about," I replied. She was still mad about me telling on her friend. This was ridiculous.

"Valerie, why are you trippin'? I said I was sorry. I didn't know it was some big secret. How many times do I have to tell you that? I mean, the way that you're acting, you act like you're the long lost daughter and not your friend."

As soon as the words left my mouth, a light bulb went off, confirmed by the fact that Valerie lost her smile and tears began to fill her eyes.

"You're not so dumb after all," she said, sounding like some kind of zombie.

"Wh-what?" My mouth dropped open. "You're Glenda Matthews's daughter?"

She stepped forward and I stepped back.

"Yes, I'm the unwanted child of the world's biggest superstar," she said sadly, but then quickly forced a smile. "But I wasn't sweatin' it. Yeah, I would get jealous of Sheridan and her life every now and then, but I have a good family. I have a mother and father that adopted this poor little orphan. But they love me very much. And Glenda Matthews has set up a nice little trust fund that I'll get when I turn eighteen, provided the story never gets out."

I just wasn't understanding. "Then why did you tell me?"

She slammed the table. That's when I noticed the long butcher knife in her hand. "I told you because I was sharing with you! I wanted to be your friend!" she yelled. "I thought I could trust you."

I wanted to ask why she would think that when we barely

knew one another. But she had started wildly waving the knife so now definitely wasn't the time for questions.

I felt like ice was running through my veins as I backed up slowly. "Okay, Valerie, chill."

"Don't tell me to chill!" She jabbed the knife my way. "How did you even find out it was me?"

"I didn't know," I said. "I just made that up."

"You liar!"

I held up my hands in defense. "No, seriously, I just said that because I thought it was Sheridan who was stalking me. I wanted to freak her out."

"Ha, like Sheridan's ditzy behind would be able to set you up so smoothly."

"So you were behind everything?" I asked in disbelief. "Sheridan didn't have anything to do with it?"

"No, you idiot! Sheridan wasn't smart enough to play you like I did!"

I couldn't believe I'd let my guard down so much to have this psycho that close to me. But right now, it was all about convincing her that I didn't know anything.

"Valerie, I promise, I wasn't meeting anyone," I said, calmly. "I just wanted to make Sheridan think I was. Please. just let me go. I'll pretend this never happened."

She thrust the knife toward me again. "You think I trust you now? You think I believe anything that comes out of your lying mouth?" she screamed, spit flying out of her mouth. "No, there's only one way to shut you up."

"Please, Valerie, I'm sorry. Just leave and I'll forget this ever happened and I'll drop the story."

"I risked everything, trying to share with you," she cried. "My mom was so mad at me. She's never been that mad at me. Glenda has threatened to take all my money. And for what? Because you just had to do the freakin' story. Do you think I would ever trust you again?"

"Look, I'm sorry. I had no idea."

"I asked you to let it go," she cried.

"You should've just told me it was you and I would've dropped it." I glanced at the door trying to gauge how I could make a run for it.

"You expect me to believe that?" She caught me eyeing the door and immediately lunged at me. I ducked out of the way as the knife came down, but she grabbed my leg as I tried to scramble away. We wrestled and I scurried out of the way, screaming for help.

"There's no one here to help you," she yelled as she jerked me toward her.

I tried to get to the phone, but she kicked it out of my reach.

"What do you want from me?" I cried as she pinned me down. "I told you, I won't do the show."

"I don't believe you!"

I didn't know who this psycho was. She was raging out of control as she put the knife up against my throat. I just knew I was about to die. I closed my eyes, saying a silent prayer. I so didn't want to go out like this. But I stopped fighting her because it was like she had some superhuman strength. I felt myself giving up and then I heard someone yell, "Valerie!"

I saw Bryce standing there and wanted to scream tears of joy at the sight of him. Valerie paused long enough to look toward the voice. That gave Bryce enough time to tackle her and knock the knife out of her hand. But she kicked him squarely between the legs and he doubled over in pain and she scrambled for the knife. She'd just grabbed it when Sheridan yelled, "Stop! Don't. Valerie, you don't want to do this."

I was shocked to see Sheridan, but I used the reprieve to get out of the way.

Valerie looked surprised to see her. "You don't know what I want to do," she yelled.

"I do know," she said calmly. "I promise I do."

"You don't know anything about me."

"I know that you're my half sister," Sheridan whispered.

"What?" Valerie said, stopping in her tracks. "H-how long have you known?"

"Just a couple of days. My mom told me. She was scared it may come out. So, she wanted me to hear it from her." Sheridan looked at the knife, then back up at Valerie. "You don't want to do this. She's not worth it."

Valerie started shaking. "She's ruined everything! My parents are so angry with me. My money is gone. Glenda sent my mother a letter saying they'd violated the agreement, so I wouldn't get my money."

"No, it's not gone," Sheridan said. She held up her arm to hold Bryce back as he'd finally pulled himself up off the floor and was struggling to walk over toward us. The expression on Sheridan's face begged him to let her handle this.

Bryce looked at me and my eyes told him to listen to Sheridan. Right about now, Sheridan seemed to be our only hope to rein in this maniac.

"I assure you, I won't let my mom take your money," Sheridan said.

Valerie looked like she wanted to desperately believe her.

Sheridan turned to me. "I know Maya has a big mouth, but I can promise you she won't do this story. It's all going to go away. No one will ever know."

Valerie glanced over at me like she didn't trust me.

I didn't know what would happen tomorrow, but right about now I would say whatever I needed to say to get the heck out of here, so I nodded and said, "She's right. I won't."

Valerie studied me for a minute, then dropped the knife, buried her face in her hands, and sobbed.

Chapter 54

I took a deep breath as I walked into the conference room. I knew the producing team at WSVV was expecting me to deliver. I had Valerie's photo and the video tape in a manila envelope. I'd thought long and hard about revealing Glenda Matthews's daughter's identity, but this story was too good to pass up. Yeah, I know what I'd said, but at the end of the day, I had to do what I had to do.

"Come on in," Tamara said when she spotted me at the door. She waved me in excitedly, then pointed at the chair at the end of the conference room table. "I've been telling them all how psyched you are about this blockbuster story so we know it has to be good."

"Is it about Erin Anderson, the actress? Because I heard some rumors that she got into a brawl last week downtown after using a racial slur against a waitress. Apparently, she paid the waitress off," Ken said.

"Please tell me it's about Glenda Matthews. You got some more dirt on her," Dexter interjected. He turned to Tamara. "That show got the network the highest rating ever so we need to keep the momentum going."

My stomach churned as I sat down. I could definitely get the ratings with this Lifetime movie that unfolded yesterday.

"Oh, yes, please let it be about Glenda," Ken added. "Erin can wait!"

"Would you guys be quiet and let her tell us," Tamara playfully snapped.

Valerie's face flashed before my eyes and for the first time, I wondered what it must've felt like for her. How did it feel growing up in Sheridan's shadow? What must it have felt like to know that your mother had chosen a movie over you? And how could she carry that secret?

I still couldn't believe Valerie was behind everything. The notes, the emails, even paying the two thugs to rough me up. Apparently, she'd had a lapse in judgment in sharing her secret with me and truly regretted it. Then, she'd been willing to go to any lengths to shut me up.

"So, come on, Maya, spill it," Dexter said, interrupting my thoughts.

I reached into my bag and pulled out the manila envelope and pushed it toward them. All three of them reached for it at the same time. Tamara grabbed it first and tore it open. She frowned, then turned the picture around to me.

"Wh-what in the world is this?" she asked.

"What does it look like?"

"It looks like a man dressed up in a woman's mini-skirt and heels," she replied.

"That man is the vice-principal of a local high school."

"Is he a celebrity?" Ken asked, leaning in and frowning as he looked at the photo.

I shrugged. "No, but that's all I have."

"*This* was your blockbuster story?" Tamara asked in disbelief.

"You don't think that's a big story?" I replied, trying to act offended.

"Maybe for a mainstream news station," Dexter said, taking the photo from Tamara. He also stared at it like he couldn't believe this was it.

"Yeah, he's not a celebrity," Ken said. "So why do we care?"

"Our motto is 'where we dish the dirt on your favorite celebrities,' " Dexter said. "Nobody cares about some high school vice principal."

I acted like I was disappointed. "Sorry, that's all I got."

Tamara inhaled. "Maya, this is not going to work."

"Look," I said, before she could even get started. I was tired of playing games and wanted to just tell them what I really felt. "I like this job. I really do, but if I'm going to keep doing it, I'm going to have to go digging for dirt in someone else's backyard. All of this I've been doing just hits too close to home."

Dexter groaned. "Here we go again. Maybe we should call Sheridan after all."

"Maybe you should," I replied. That hurt my heart, but I refused to let them see it. All three of them looked at me in shock.

As much as I wanted this job, I'd seen what my actions had done to Valerie and I actually kinda liked the nerd. And I felt bad. Not bad enough to quit, but bad enough to stop spilling the goods on my friends.

"I'm sure this is disappointing to you," I said, standing. My dad had taught me the art of bluffing and yeah, I might have only been seventeen, but I was mastering it well.

"So, you talk among yourselves and let me know what you want to do. I'm cool either way." I flashed a forced smile and said a silent prayer that they didn't call my bluff because honestly, I loved my job.

I gathered my purse, made sure the photo of Valerie was tucked safely inside, and left the building.

I had just made my way into the parking lot when I noticed Sheridan across the street leaned up against her silver Mercedes. Instead of going to my car, I walked across the street. She was standing there, her arms folded, tears in her eyes.

"So, I guess you're going to get your blockbuster ratings?" she said, sadly.

"I already have blockbuster ratings," I said. I opened my purse, reached in, and handed her Valerie's envelope. "I don't need to try and build them anymore."

She was apprehensive as she took the envelope. "What is this?"

"Open it."

She slowly did so as I continued. "That's the video I had rolling at the cabin."

"You were taping it?"

I smiled. "I was hoping to catch you in the act of stalking me."

Her mouth dropped opened in disbelief. "You thought *I* was the stalker? Like seriously?"

I nodded. "Yeah, especially after I saw you talking to Jennifer Graham." I didn't want to admit to having taped them in the locker room. "Valerie had said Jenn's mom was how she found out everything. I thought you were working with her."

Sheridan scrunched up her nose. "I was. On my research paper. She wrote my paper for history and I was trying to get her to do it for English, too. But you know she's all Dolly Do-Right and didn't want to do it. So, she told me I was on my own."

I couldn't help but chuckle. They'd been talking about schoolwork? Yeah, good thing I didn't go to the cops.

Sheridan looked at the photo of Valerie and cupped the tape tightly. "Is this the only copy?"

I nodded. "It is."

She finally laughed. It was more like a sigh of relief. "I can't believe you thought I was stalking you. Oh, I was mad at your janky behind, but I'm not going to waste my time stalking anyone. You of all people should know I don't roll like that. Yeah, I sent the pictures, and I'm sorry, but that was only because the opportunity fell in my lap. I'm not wasting time trying to terrorize you."

I looked at the girl who had been my best friend for years. If I really thought about it, I guess I did know that about Sheridan. A lot of time, thought, and effort had gone into stalking me and I should've known Sheridan wasn't going to go to such extremes.

Sheridan sighed as her eyes watered. "Thank you," she said, pulling the envelope close to her chest.

"So, Valerie's your half sister?" I asked. I'd been up all night processing that information. Bryce had immediately gotten me out of the beach house. I could only assume Sheridan had made sure she got home.

Sheridan nodded. "My mom told me right after your story," she admitted. "But it wasn't until yesterday at the mall that her mom called me, concerned that she was going to do something drastic. Apparently, she'd left a message that she was going to take care of you and make it right."

Take care of me. That sent chills up my spine.

"Since I knew she was listening when Bryce told me you were going to the beach house, I knew that's where she was headed," Sheridan said.

I stared at my former BFF. I was so grateful that she'd decided to come try and stop Valerie, because she could've gone on about her business. And there's no telling how things would've ended.

"So, what's gonna happen with Valerie?" I asked.

"My mom won't go see her," Sheridan said sadly. "She said that part of her life is closed. She made a mistake, as she says, and doesn't want to revisit it. It's really jacked up."

"Wow" was all I could say. "What about you? How are you taking the news?"

Sheridan shrugged and softly said, "I don't know, having a nerd for a sister. You know, I have to get used to that idea."

"Maybe you can teach her a thing or two."

"Maybe," Sheridan said. "But I called this morning to check on her and she said something about her parents moving her away. So, I don't know what's going to happen."

We stood in an awkward silence for a moment before Sheridan added, "Maya, maybe you can one day forgive me for being such a jerk. All the stuff that went down with Bryce. I don't even like him like that." She lowered her head in shame. "I just wanted to hurt you. I'm sorry."

I think in the entire time I'd known Sheridan, I could count on one hand the number of times she'd apologized to anyone so the fact that she'd apologized to me was major.

"Maybe" was all I could say. We stood in silence again, before she finally said, "So what's going to happen with your show?"

I shrugged. "I hope that I can keep doing it, but I will have to change a few things."

"Like selling out your friends?"

I smiled. "Yeah, like selling out my friends." This was all getting way too deep so I added, "Who knows, maybe I could bring you on as a sidekick."

She raised one eyebrow. "Oh, don't get it twisted. Sheridan Matthews is nobody's sidekick."

I laughed because that was such a Maya Morgan answer.

"Well, I have to get going."

We said our good-byes and I headed back to the car. I couldn't see the station getting rid of me. And if they did, someone else would pick me up and give me a show. After all, I was Maya Morgan.

I climbed into my car, looked in the rearview mirror and blew a kiss at my reflection. "Yep, I'm still the bomb-dot-com. And these folks better recognize," I mumbled, before popping on my Chanel glasses and heading home.

RUMOR CENTRAL

ReShonda Tate Billingsley

ABOUT THIS GUIDE

The following questions are intended to
enhance your group's reading of
RUMOR CENTRAL.

DISCUSSION QUESTIONS

1. Maya's friends felt like she sold them out when she accepted her own show. Do you agree? How would you have handled the situation?

2. Valerie said she was just sharing the news about Sheridan's mother because she thought she and Maya were friends. Do you think she should've told Maya in the first place? Was Maya wrong for using that information?

3. Maya felt like Sheridan crossed a line when she got with Bryce. What do you think about what Sheridan did? Should Maya have forgiven her?

4. Maya sent provocative pictures to Bryce, thinking no one else would ever see them. Who do you think is to blame for the pictures going viral? Do you know anyone who has ever done something like this?

5. What do you think about the way Maya and her friends treated the scholarship kids?

6. Could you dig up dirt and spread gossip on your friends if it meant you could get fame and fortune?

In stores now!

Hollywood High: Get Ready for War
by Ni-Ni Simone and Amir Abrams

Welcome to Hollywood High, where socialites rule
and popularity is more of a drug than designer digs
could ever be . . .

Turn the page for an excerpt from *Get Ready for War.* . . .

Who needed enemies when you had hatin' media and bloggers maliciously tearing you up every chance they got and a bunch of selfish, backstabbers as friends.

Oh no. My enemies weren't the ones I needed to keep my mink-lashed eyes on. It was the Pampered Princesses of Hollywood High Academy who kept me dragged into their shenanigans, along with the paparazzi that lived and breathed to destroy me. Hence why I was wearing a floppy hat and hiding behind a pair of ostrich-leather Moss Lipow sunglasses.

I was a trendsetter.

A shaker 'n' mover.

A fashionista extraordinaire.

I was London Phillips.

Not a joke!

And my name had no business being caught up in any of the most recent scandals with Heather's (aka Wu-Wu) Skittles fest. If she wanted to overdose on her granny's heart medicine, then she needed to leave me out of it.

My reputation of being fine, fly, and eternally fabulous was etched on the pages of magazines and carved in the minds of many. And I was one of the most adored, envied, and hated for all of my divaliciousness. It came with the territory of being deliciously beautiful. And I embraced it.

But being on top didn't mean a thing if you didn't know how to stay there. Reputation was everything at Hollywood High. And up until three days ago, I was perched up on Mt. Everest in all of my fabulousness, looking down at any- and everyone who followed me or aspired to be me, but could (or would) *never* be me. Yeah, it had been a cold-blooded climb to the top. But so what? A diva did what she had to do to get what she wanted and needed. And I had made it.

But I wasn't in New York anymore, reigning alone. No. I was in Hollywood. And I had to share the mountaintop with three skanks who were supposed to be the "It Clique." And they had been. *And we had been.* But now we were about to lose our crowns as the Pampered Princesses of Hollywood High if Heather, Spencer, and Rich didn't get it together— quick, fast, and in a hurry. Their antics were destroying my reputation. And theirs!

The media and bloggers were having a field day tearing us up in the headlines. Kicking us in our crowns and branding us last week's hot trash. Not respecting that we were the daughters of high-profiled celebrities. Naming us this week's flops. They really thought we had fallen off our white-horsed carriages. And from the looks of things, we had. Here I was, again, in the midst of Rich, Spencer, and Heather's bull. But enough was enough.

I was determined to handle Rich first. I had to get her focused. But this wench, who I thought was easy and gullible, wasn't playing along the way I thought. No, she was too busy chasing behind some boy whom she seemed obsessed with being with. And that was a problem—for *me!*

Shoot. Can I get my life?

As I walked through the school's café doors, pulling out

my cell, it was eerily quiet, but I had no time to figure out why. I needed to get in touch with Rich. Where r you?

A string-bean-thin girl with a pink-and-black Mohawk, black eyeliner, and black lipstick stepped up to me and handed me a FREE WU-WU T-shirt being distributed by Wu-Wu's many stalkers, gawkers, and fanatics. I stared the walking toothpick down. "Beanpole, who told you you could get up in my space?" I snapped, tossing the shirt in her face. "Go hang yourself with it. And make sure you get it right."

Her eyes popped open.

I was sooooo not in the mood. I needed to know where Rich and Spencer were. I already knew where Heather's wretched self was. But Rich and Spencer were both unaccounted for. This made the fifteenth time I had pulled out my phone today to check for any messages or missed calls from Rich because I had been calling her and texting her and leaving her messages since seven o'clock this morning. Sweating her; something I don't do. And still there was nothing from her.

Zilch.

Nada.

As I was walking and texting Rich another where-are-you message, I couldn't help but notice the noise level in the café. Normally it was full of chatter and laughter and all types of music.

Not today.

Dead silence.

All I heard was a bunch of clicking from cameras. And a few comments like "Uh-oh, it's about to go down now" as I made my way farther into the center of the café. Suddenly I knew what all of the silence was about. There was a group of girls sitting at our table. You know. The one that has, or had, the pink tablecloth and a humungous RESERVED FOR THE PAMPERED PRINCESSES sign up on it. Yeah, that table.

Screech!

Everyone knew on this side of campus that the Pampered Princesses were the ruling clique. And no one sat at our table. No one!

I pulled up the rim of my hat, inched my shades down to the tip of my nose, and peered at them.

I blinked.

I couldn't believe what I was seeing. The group of girls had on uniforms. And judging by the colors, I knew they absolutely did not belong on this side of the campus.

This has to be a mistake.

I marched over toward them, then stood and stared at the group of chicks who had foolishly parked their behinds and taken up space at our table. These preemies had *our* table covered with a fuchsia tablecloth. And they had the nerve to have the table set with fine china and a candelabra in the center of the table, as if they were preparing for some kind of holiday feast. And they sat pretty as they pleased, as if they owned the room.

They all wore their hair pulled back into sleek, shiny ponytails with colorful jeweled clips. I ice-grilled them, expecting them to scatter like frightened roaches. Not! They didn't budge. Didn't even blink an eyelash. Nope, those munchkin critters defiantly stayed planted in their seats and continued on with their chatter as if I didn't exist. And at that very moment, I felt like the whole cafeteria had zoomed in on me. I quickly glanced around the room to assess the situation. They had. And it was turning into a nightmare. All eyes were clearly on me! Cameras clicked.

I cleared my throat.

They continued talking and laughing.

Did they come here to bring it?

If I wasn't so peeved at their disrespect, I would have been impressed. And truth is, they were adorable. But that was not the time, nor the place, to give props to a bunch of bratty

Beanie Babies trying to serve me drama. I had enough of that with my own clique, so I sure wasn't going to tolerate it from a bunch of ninth-grade peons in navy blazers, green-and-blue plaid pleated skirts, and black Nine West pumps.

I picked up a fork from off the table and tapped one of the glasses with it. "Umm, excuse you. Excuse you, excuse you."

The chick sitting at the far end of the table craned her neck in my direction and stared me down. She had beautiful skin and an oversized forehead. "The name's Harlow. H-A-R-L-O-W. And whaaat? You want my autograph? 'Cause I don't do groupies."

Oh no, now I knew that them being at our table was not a mistake. Those tricklets had strutted over to this side of the campus purposely to bring it. All in the name of getting it crunked.

Now, along with the media, we had teenybopper freshmen trying to bring it to us!

They really don't want it. Apparently they don't know what they're asking for.

I took a deep breath. Determined to keep it cute, calm, and collected. I couldn't afford to dish out another hundred grand for tearing up the café, again. Daddy would kill me for sure. "Sweetie, I don't know who misplaced your lunch period, and I'm sure this is your nap time. But this right here"—I patted the table—"is not for you."

She smirked. "And you are?"

I tilted my head. "About to become your worst nightmare in a minute if you-all don't get up from this table."

The four of them stared at each other, then looked around as if they were searching for something. "Umm, excuse me, Starlets," the Harlow chick said to her little Cheerios crew. "Do any of you see a name tag with the name Buffalo Hips on it?"

"Creature from the wild . . ." the three others sang out.

"Is looking for someplace to sit," a golden-brown chick sitting next to Harlow added.

Stay calm.

Just relax.

Let me try this again.

"Umm, where's your babysitter? Because apparently there's been an escape from the nursery; toddlers gone wild . . ."

"Umm, excuse me, Miss London," one of the white-gloved servers said, coming to the table with two trays. I blinked. He set a platter of burgers and milk shakes in the center of the table, then walked off, eyeing me.

Then those little disrespectful chicks had the nerve to snap open their napkins and lay them neatly on their laps.

Oh, this had gone too far!

I placed a hand up on my hip and tossed my Fendi hobo bag in the center of the table, disrupting everything on it. They jumped.

"Eww . . ."

"Ohmygod . . ."

"Did someone dump their garbage here? How gross is that."

"Isn't that last year's bag?"

"Exaaaactly, Arabia," Miss Forehead said, tossing her ponytail. "Old head's tryna serve us. Now get your fashion right."

Wait. Did Forehead just call me an old head?

They waved their arms up in the air and snapped. "Mmmph, exaaaaactly."

The other two sitting across from Harlow and the Arabia chick snickered, like two cackling backup singers. They really didn't understand. I was trying to spare them from a beatdown. Truth is they reminded me of me, and my old clique back in New York when we were their age. But that was then. And this was now! Still, they had heart. And they were sassy. Their diamonds sparkled. And one of them I knew for sure had money. I could smell it all over her. But that had nothing to do with all four of them being totally out of line.

I leaned in and spoke real tight-lipped. "I don't know if you four little bimbos are trying to be cute, or intentionally trying to work me over, or if you simply banged your over-sized foreheads on the monkey bars during recess, but obviously you all missed the memo on which clique reigned supreme here."

They burst out laughing all hard and crazy, then stopped abruptly. "Hmmm"—they snapped their fingers—"Not!"

The Harlow chick turned to me and said, "No, ma'am, we didn't miss the memo. We didn't miss the blogs either. Let's see. If we're not mistaken, they all say"—she glanced over at her posse—"drum roll, please . . ."

"Losers!" they shouted in unison.

The cafeteria erupted in laughter.

My face was cracked. I couldn't believe that a pack of toddlers in cheesy uniforms were trying to set it off and disrespect *me* to my face. Cute girls or not, this was a problem!

Cameras continued clicking.

The Harlow chick was clearly Miss Mouth Almighty—and the appointed ringleader. "Page twenty-seven in *Hot or Not* magazine"—she started flipping through the tabloid—"says that the Pampered Princesses have fallen apart." She eyed me, putting a hand up to her chest. "Oooh, look at Heather . . ."

"Junkie," they sang out.

Another said, "Aaah, Wu-Wu's in the house."

"Not!" they all said, snapping their fingers again.

Harlow continued. "Black beauties, baby . . ."

"Crushed and ready to go . . ." the backup singers sang out. "Got it on lock . . ."

The Arabia chick said. "Oooh-oooh . . . don't forget about the fakest of 'em all."

"Who, Rich?" Harlow smirked.

"Boom bop, make it drop," they all said in unison. "Pop pop, get it, get it . . ."

"Yeah, a baby," Harlow sneered.

"Clutching pearls, clutching pearls," her three cheerleaders mocked, placing a hand up to their necks.

The café went wild.

It was clear that these girls had been watching us hard. *Mmmph, even the young broads trying to jock our spots.*

Harlow rolled her eyes. "Oh, puhleeeeeze. How tired is that? *Clutching pearls.* Who says that?"

"Has-beens," one of her giggling sidekicks snorted.

"Mmmm, exaaaaactly!" Harlow and the Arabia chick snapped.

"Oh, wait," Harlow stated excitedly, clapping her hands together. "Let's not forget Spencer . . ."

"The dizzy chick," they said. "Smells like cat pee . . . smells like cat pee . . ."

"Somewhere . . ."

"Down on her knees. Down on her knees," they all chimed in.

"Mopping the floor and making videos," Arabia added.

"Nine-one-one, this is an emergency . . . this is an emergency . . ."

I was hot! Rich was somewhere knocked up, Heather was somewhere drugged up or going through withdrawals, and Spencer was probably somewhere neck bobbing. And, once again, I was the one getting dragged—*alone!*

Harlow eyed me up and down, curling her lips up into a dirty sneer. "And you, London . . ."

Ohhhhkay, here we go!

"Freak!" they all yelled out in unison. "Caught up in the matrix . . . Caught up in the matrix . . ."

I blinked.

And before I could catch myself, before she could get the rest of her sentence finished, I backhanded her so hard she fell backward. And spit slung from her mouth. They all screamed as I swung that little Gerber baby around the café and gave her the beatdown of her life. Then, in the midst of all the cameras clicking and tables being tossed up, the other three Romper Room hookers jumped up on my back and tackled me to the floor. And the only thing I could think about was being stomped down by a bunch of Crenshaw Crippettes in cheap, pleather pumps. *This was a state of emergency!*

I was clearly behind enemy lines. And it was all Rich's, Spencer's, and Heather's fault because they didn't know how to handle their scandal.